HUGE X4

A DOUBLE TWIN STEPBROTHER
MMFMM REVERSE HAREM ROMANCE

STEPHANIE BROTHER

Copyright © 2017 STEPHANIE BROTHER

All Rights Reserved. This book or any portion thereof may not be reproduced or used in any manner whatsoever without the express permission of the publisher except for the use of brief quotations in a book review.

This book is a work of fiction. Any resemblance to persons, living or dead, or places, events or locations is purely coincidental. The characters are all productions of the author's imagination.

Please note that this work is intended only for adults over the age of 18 and all characters represented as 18 or over.

ISBN: 9781091135581

CONTENTS

1	White lace and emptiness	1
2	Cocktails and games	10
3	Dancing my way to happiness	21
4	Finding paradise	29
5	Morning glory	45
6	Bed and breakfast	54
7	Mixed doubles	63
8	Beach babes	70
9	Double bubble burst	78
10	Rude awakening	90
11	Spotless mind	95
12	Double disappointment	108
13	Running into trouble	120
14	Room with a view	126

15	Home isn't where the heart is	132
16	Knights in white T-shirts	145
17	A sisterly awakening	156
18	Revenge and reward	168
19	Caught between four rock hard places	176
EPILOGUE	4X the happiness	194

1

WHITE LACE AND EMPTINESS

It's a big day for Kerry. A new beginning. A wedding day that two years ago we never imagined she would be preparing for. Life is funny like that. Even after experiencing terrible things, love can sneak up on you and make you whole again. At least, that's what Kerry told me last night as we shared some champagne and I helped her resist the urge to break tradition and seek out her husband-to-be the night before the wedding. Did I believe her? It was hard not to. Life had knocked her down hard, but it had sent her Dean to raise her up again.

My sister emerges from the bathroom, make-up done to perfection, wearing just the underwear she'd spent hours picking out in Macy's. She looks amazing.

"Wow," I say, shaking my head.

"Not bad for an old girl." She spins around laughing and for a second she morphs into teenage Kerry, wild and carefree. I want to join her so badly but I'm coiled too tightly; too used to holding myself back so I don't embarrass anybody, most of all myself.

"Thirty is hardly old. You want me to help you into your dress?"

She shakes her head. "I'll be okay."

I nod once and walk over to the wardrobe to undo the dress carrier. The zip slips down as smoothly as a knife through soft butter and I peel back the course black fabric to reveal the soft tulle beneath.

"It's so beautiful," I say, slipping it from the hanger and taking it to my sister.

"It was the first one I saw. I wanted it to be completely different from the last one." For a moment her face seems to freeze. It's natural, I suppose, that she'd think of her first wedding at this moment. Most of us hope that we won't be repeating that day in our lifetimes, but when you're made a widow in your twenties it's kind of inevitable.

"It's okay to think about it," I tell her. "It's okay to feel a little wistful for that day too. Just because you've met someone new, doesn't mean it has to wipe away the past."

Kerry smiles at me. "I feel as happy today as I felt the first time. That's good, isn't it?"

I give her arm a squeeze. "Of course it is."

She smiles brusquely, as though she's swallowing back the memories to focus on the present day.

I head back over to the closet and take my dress down. It's a pretty silk tea dress that we chose together on one of our many shopping trips. I slide off my robe and pull it on, enjoying the soft slip of it against my skin. It takes time to fasten all the little buttons but it's worth it for the effect. By the time I'm done, Kerry is ready too.

"Will you help me with my shoes?" she asks.

"Sure." I kneel at her feet and slip on her white satin shoes, fastening the buckle at each side. I smile up at her when I'm done. She looks like an angel in her ethereal dress with the Caribbean sun streaming through the window behind her.

"You'll find someone too, you know," Kerry says softly.

I shake my head because I don't want to go there. Not now when my face is made up and I have my carefully crafted smile fixed in place.

"Brad was a douchebag. Nobody liked him, sweetie. You deserve so much more."

"I know," I say, standing quickly and fussing with my dress to cover up my discomfort. Although it's been months since I left him, it still feels raw. There's still a big hole in my heart where he carved out his space until I didn't know left from right or up from down. "Come on," I say. "Dean will be waiting."

Kerry's eyes are bright as we gather our final things together. She takes hold of my hand as we make our way from her honeymoon suite to the outdoor venue where the guests have congregated. Our father left when we were young, and although mom loves the limelight, Kerry had insisted that it be me to give her away. That wasn't received well by mom but Kerry has always been braver about standing up to her than I have.

"You know that the O'Connell twins arrived last night," Kerry says.

"Oh, thank goodness," I say squeezing her hand. Dean's two best friends, Callum and Liam, who were flying in from Dubai had their flights canceled and were looking at alternative routes to make it in time. "Dean must be so happy."

"He is. It wouldn't have been the same for him if they weren't here to stand with him."

"It's a little unorthodox having two best men," I say.

"Well, they've all been friends since college," Kerry says. "Plus they're identical twins so they're used to doing things together!"

As we get closer she squeezes my hand tightly and pulls me to a stop. Her eyes are bright when she puts her hands on my cheeks. "Promise me that you'll make the most of your time here," she says. "You've been hiding away for so long. It's time to come out of your shell again, sweetie. Don't let opportunities pass you by anymore."

I blink, trying not to get emotional. Before we came here she'd sent me a notebook with the words 'Don't ever let anyone steal your sparkle' on the cover in silver glittery cursive. I carry it everywhere with me as a reminder. Funny, because I don't feel like my sparkle has returned yet so there's going to be no 'giving it away' in the foreseeable future. "I will," I tell her but she shakes her head.

"I don't believe you when you say it in that reluctant way of yours. Brad is gone. The only person holding you back now is you. And ignore mom, okay? She's been like herself but on speed since we got here…you know she's gonna say some stuff that's gonna be insensitive because that's just what she does."

She smiles at me and kisses me on my right cheek and I pull her into the tightest hug possible without creasing both of our dresses.

"I love you, Sis."

"I know, sweetie. I love you too."

We draw apart and I smile with genuine feeling this time. "Come on. Let's go make an honest woman out of you."

"Funny," Kerry says, but she's so ready to get to Dean that we are practically skipping towards the sea.

Kerry and Dean have chosen to get married outside on a grassy spot looking out over the ocean. A small group of friends and family sit awaiting our arrival. A single musician plays a soft melody. At the front, Dean faces the other away, but as the congregation stands he turns to see his bride.

I know I shouldn't feel jealous of my sister. She's an amazing woman who has been through so much and deserves all the love that this man has pouring from his eyes. But I am envious. No one has ever looked at me the way he looks at her, and I want it. I want it so badly that it's physically painful; a clenching in my gut and heart that makes me want to fold in two and crumple to the ground. I don't, though. I pull myself as straight as I can, head held high, and I walk my big sister to where her knight in white linen is waiting for her. All eyes are on us, and I look to find Dean's best men, who until now have just been the stuff of intriguing stories.

Two broad backs in crisp white shirts, dark hair cropped short at the nape and a little longer on the top. They turn and I'm hit by four intense gray eyes that are made even more spectacular because they are framed by thick dark lashes. I see them taking in Kerry first, smiling broadly. Then both their gazes move to me and I'm mesmerized. If I wasn't currently holding on to Kerry's arm and being propelled along by her eagerness to join her husband-to-be, I'd probably have been fixed to the spot. I blow out my breath because the fluttery feeling in my tummy isn't something I'm used to. I don't remember the last time I was hit with such a wave of attraction. It's like a lightning bolt or a tidal wave. I blink slowly and watch as their smiles widen. I should smile back. I know I should but my face isn't cooperating. I'm sure I look like a frightened deer and that is not a good look for a maid of honor.

Maid. I wince at the thought. Kerry is about to say vows for the second time and I still haven't achieved my first. I feel my sister squeeze my arm and I catch her looking at me and smiling. I beam back because she looks so full of hope and joy and it's at least partly contagious.

At the front, she pauses so that I can take her bouquet and then Dean is there, reaching for her hand, cradling it like it's a precious and fragile bird. I stand next to Kerry to witness her commit her life to Dean. Liam and Callum stand next to Dean to do the same.

The officiant makes quick work of the ceremony. One of the twins hands over the rings at the appropriate time and my mind drifts, taking in the turquoise sea that spreads in front of us like a glittering carpet. I can't imagine a more perfect place to get married.

It's over so quickly I almost don't realize until the crowd begins to clap and I turn to find Kerry and Dean engaging in a very loving 'first kiss'. Behind them, Callum and Liam are smiling at the happy couple, then they both look up and grin at me. Two sets of amazing white teeth almost blind me. It's like looking into the sun and I blink slowly, feeling totally weak in the knees.

Kerry and Dean turn to the crowd and everyone begins to cheer. Before they make their way down the grassy path between the white chairs, she turns to reclaim her bouquet. It's then that I realize I am going to have to walk behind her, flanked by two intimidatingly good-looking best men. I don't get a chance to think about how I might avoid it. Twin one is there, taking my left hand and slipping it through his arm. I look down at where our bodies are now touching. Then, before I have a chance to respond, twin two is at my right doing the same thing. The soloist increases the tempo of the music and we all parade back down the aisle.

I know my cheeks are on fire. I can feel the blood tingling at the surface. It's so ridiculous to be embarrassed simply because I'm innocently touching two of Dean's best friends, but I can't help it. I don't know these men and they are unnervingly good-looking and confident in a way that makes me feel small and pathetic.

"You're Bethany," one of them says gently as we make our way towards the place the photographer has set up for the formal photographs. I nod because my tongue is also a traitor. "I'm Liam," he says. "That's Callum." He nods towards his brother and I glance over and nod too. God, this is awful. I'm cringing and embarrassed and I just want this part to be over so that I can go and hide at the wedding reception and busy myself with the buffet and a triple gin and tonic. I know it's not classy to get drunk at your sister's wedding but somehow it seems like the only way I might get through this day in one piece.

"I'll bet Dean is glad you made it in time," I say when I manage to make conversation.

"Yeah," Callum says. "We nearly didn't. It was almost like something was working against us."

"We were worried about getting on a plane by the time we found a route to get here. So much had gone wrong. It almost felt like a sign."

"But you're here in one piece," I say.

"Two pieces." Callum sniggers and I blush again. I'm going to need to start introducing myself as beetroot-head before long.

"I think Bethany probably noticed that about us already," Liam says in an almost scolding voice.

"You'll have to excuse me if I get you confused," I say.

"You won't be the first," Callum says.

"Or the last," Liam adds.

"Can I tell you a secret?" Callum leans in closer as though he intends to whisper something directly into my ear, and I get a nose full of a delicious-smelling cologne rising off warm skin. I nod because I'm feeling dazed. "Liam has a little scar on his forehead. That's how you can tell us apart."

Liam leans in close to catch the end of Callum's confession and sniggers. "There are other ways to tell us apart," he murmurs, "but we'd have to take our clothes off for that."

A shiver runs up my spine as I turn and am caught in his gaze. I don't know what to say. Dark and dirty thoughts flash through my mind of two gorgeous men standing naked before me. What differences might they have? Scars? Birthmarks? Maybe something naughtier. My cheeks feel warm and Liam leans in even closer. "I think you know what I mean."

I inhale deeply; a shuddering breath that is part nervous and part aroused. I mean, how could I not be? They smell so good and their voices are low with a slight husky edge that is just dripping with sex.

It's been such a long time since I thought about sex. Feeling worthless and down kills any kind of desire. I wasn't expecting to be feeling like this now at my sister's wedding, and certainly not about two men. I seriously must be losing my mind. Maybe it's the sun. I was at the beach for a long time yesterday. It could be sunstroke.

"Are you okay?" Callum asks.

I nod and Liam chuckles. "I think she's blown a fuse!"

I look between them and snap myself back into reality. I'm here for Kerry. She needs me to keep my mind on the job. Maid of Honor extraordinaire. "We need to go over there for the photos," I say, and walk away, leaving them behind me.

2
COCKTAILS AND GAMES

The photo shoot is painful, not because I'm conscious of having my picture taken but because it's hot, and when I'm not required, I don't know where to put myself. Callum and Liam are standing on the opposite side of the photographer, so I end up catching eyes with one or both of them way too much. Every time it's like the slide of warm hot chocolate to my insides. Every time they grin at me with wickedness dripping from their mouths, I exhale a shuddery breath. This isn't normal. I've met twins before and they've never been like these ones. There's a synchronicity about them, as though they think with one mind, and move with one body. Their eyes always find me at the same time and they're not conferring.

When the photographer has completed all the required shots, I grab my mom's arm and practically sprint her up the path to the reception. Callum and Liam are walking not far behind and when they laugh at something Dean says, the deep rumble hits me straight between the legs.

God, I need a drink and some cool water on my wrists. And someone to put some sense into my head. That would usually be Kerry, but somehow I don't think now is the time for me to admit that I'm thinking naughty thoughts about the twin best men. She's got her own man to be thinking about and a whole party of guests to socialize with. I'm gonna need to do some of that socializing too, especially with the relatives who have turned up from far and wide.

I hit the bar, ordering mom a mimosa and myself a double gin and tonic, then we circulate to mingle with the guests. It's amazing to see the family that we haven't been in contact with for a while. Time slips past and before you know it cousins are married with kids that you've never even met. There's so much warmth that my heart melts a little. Family is everything. It's easy to take them for granted, especially when you're wrapped up in your own troubles and dramas. For the first time in a long time, I feel as though my vision has cleared and the world looks different, maybe because I'm different. It's impossible not to be shaped by your past. Bad experiences hurt parts of you that might never fully recover. They place doubts where you had none and insecurities where you were previously confident. They chip holes in your beliefs about who you are and what you are worth. People keep telling me that it's a slow process to overcome the emotional damage. I don't know if I'll ever shake off the scars Brad left behind. It's scary to think about ever letting myself trust someone again. I know I'm not ready to open my heart. There are still too many shattered pieces to glue together.

We all eat from the gorgeous buffet that the attentive wait staff set out on a long linen-covered table. Then, when the plates are cleared, it's time for dancing. Dean and Kerry both have a fascination with 80s pop music and have obviously asked the DJ to focus on that because they're up and grooving in a flash. No serious first dance, just lots of exaggerated retro moves that have us all in stitches. Most of the guests are up to join them by the end of the first song. I'm sitting at a table, nursing another gin and tonic and watching all the fun, when two large shadows loom over me.

"You wanna dance?" I gaze up to try and work out who said it. There's the little scar so it must be Liam.

I shake my head.

"You don't dance?" Callum takes hold of the chair next to me and turns it so it faces the dance floor, and drops himself onto it. Liam does the same on my left.

"I don't dance," I say, shaking my head again, just so they're clear.

"Everybody dances." They both slip down in their seats as if they're settling in for a while; long legs stretch out in front, hands rest on strong-looking thighs.

"I mean, look at that guy…" I follow the line of Liam's gaze to where my cousin Dylan is trying to bust a move, belly jiggling in time to the cheesy tune, and I can't help laughing.

"That's exactly what I'm talking about," I say firmly. "Dylan is a perfect example of why not everyone should be seen trying to move their bodies in time to music…or not in time in his case."

Callum snorts and shakes his head, turning to look at me. "Now, I agree that, like the case in front of us, some people are definitely on the lower end of the dancing spectrum, but that doesn't mean they shouldn't do it. Everyone should do it. It's fun even if you're uncoordinated." He turns to face me. "Are you uncoordinated, Bethany?"

I feel heat rushing to my cheeks, not because I am but because he's leaning in and just being in close proximity to him makes my body react. This near I can see his face in more detail; the little creases at the sides of his eyes that show he smiles often, and the flash of his pupils as they pick up the color from the ever-changing disco lights. I shake my head.

"So what is it then?"

When I don't answer he leans back in his chair and resumes watching the dancing, but with a thoughtful expression on his face.

"Everyone should dance," Liam says, taking a long sip from a very pink looking drink. "It should be a rule."

"A rule?"

"Yeah, you know. Things that just are…like respecting personal space, not burping after you've eaten…that kind of thing."

"Those sound like basic social skills, Liam."

"Well," he says shrugging, "maybe they were bad examples. You wouldn't say people shouldn't sing if they didn't have nice voices."

"Yes, I would!"

"What, even in the shower?"

"The shower's fine, but not in public."

"Ah, so you do dance but just in the privacy of your own home?"

"I'm saying nothing." I try to keep a straight face and when I glance at him out of the corner of my eye I can see him smiling.

"So anyway," Liam says, swiveling around to look at me more closely. "Who told you that you can't dance?"

"Who says someone told me?"

He narrows his eyes. "Whoever told you that is a douchebag, and everyone knows you shouldn't listen to their shit."

His gaze is intense and I can't hold it because I know he'd see the truth in my eyes. That he was right. Someone had told me I was a bad dancer and I couldn't forget it. Liam was also right that the man who had told me was a douchebag. Trouble is, when you've been in love with someone and they have managed to crawl inside your heart, it's inevitable that they worm themselves into your head too.

"So it was a gorgeous wedding, wasn't it?" I say, glancing over at where my sister is now wrapped up in her husband's embrace, holding the hem of her dress so she doesn't trip. Kerry looks so peaceful, and seeing her happy-ever-after should fill me with hope, but I've had so much of it squashed out of me.

"It was a lovely wedding," Callum says.

"They're two amazing people who deserve something good," Liam adds. "We couldn't be happier for Dean."

"I know," I sigh, hearing the wistfulness in my voice so clearly and cringing with embarrassment.

"So," Liam says, loosening his tie and rolling up his sleeves. "Back to the dancing conversation. I have a plan." There's a twinkle in his silver eyes that makes my skin feel warm, and I can't help noticing his strong tanned forearms and broad shoulders. He looks like he was involved in some kind of manly sport in his youth, maybe still is in his spare time. Callum does the same thing, and I smirk that they can't seem to remain in a position where they are different for more than a couple of seconds.

"I'm not sure I like the sound of that."

"You haven't heard what it is yet!" Callum laughs. "Give the man a chance."

"Well." Liam seems to pause for dramatic effect, or maybe he's thinking up this plan of his on the fly. "It involves alcohol. Plenty of alcohol, and a long discussion about our favorite songs. And when we've all settled on a suitable anthem, there's the opportunity to stagger across the dance floor to that strange wedding DJ over there to see if he has our song of choice."

Callum snorts. "Great plan, dude." He leans across, and they fist-bump like they're teenagers. Cue my eye-roll! I open my mouth to state my objections but Liam interrupts. "Wait a minute, pretty lady. I haven't finished yet. The deal is that if the DJ has it in his collection then we absolutely have to dance to it. If he doesn't, we'll come back here and watch all the fun. How about that? Deal?" Liam wiggles his eyebrows up and down with a huge grin plastered on his face and I burst out laughing.

"We're taking that laugh as an agreement to the proposition," Callum chuckles.

"But just to make sure…" Liam sticks out his hand to shake on it, and I hesitate, wanting to do all the fun stuff with them but not the dancing. "Come on Bethany…time's a wasting!" I hold out my hand with so much reluctance he bursts out laughing, then grabs hold of it between both of his and shakes vigorously.

"Err, you gotta shake mine too," Callum says. I turn to find it outstretched and shake it gently as well, feeling stupid and worried but a tiny bit excited too. It's that excitement that makes my throat burn a little, tears threatening. I like that feeling. It reminds me of a younger me.

"Right…drinks!"

Liam stands to scan the table, taking in the carnage of empty wine and beer bottles, then grabs my hand again and pulls me out of my seat. "We need the bar," he says, tugging me across the dance-floor, narrowly missing cousin Dylan, who's veering to one side. I turn and find Callum behind us, watching with amusement. "That man should come with a safety warning," he says as we pass through the reception room doors into the external bar area. It's quieter and brighter out here and I wonder what I look like after so many hours of maid of honor duties. My hair is probably a complete frizz as the air is humid, and I know my forehead's shiny. I curse the gods for my high maintenance appearance. Tottering on my heels as Liam comes to an abrupt halt, I rest my arms on the bar and look up at him. He's at least a foot taller than me. Ridiculous really. If I hadn't been wearing my highest heels I might have looked like a twelve-year-old kid from behind.

"So many choices," he says, grabbing the cocktail menu from where it's resting in a pool of unidentifiable liquid, and shaking it off. Callum stands next to him. "Let's see…what kind of cocktail do we think you are?" He runs his finger over the drink options as he considers them, shaking his head as he discounts the ones he deems unsuitable. "Mmm…Sex on the Beach?" Liam looks down at me from the corner of his eye. "No, I don't think so. Too sandy." I snort out a shocked laugh.

"Screaming Orgasm?" Callum's raised eyebrow is so amusing but I try not to show it on my face.

"Nah, too reserved," Liam says. I put my hands on my hips and huff but he doesn't seem fazed, switching his attention back to the menu again. "Ah…I've got it!" The twins look at each other and I stand on my tiptoes, trying to see what's being pointed at but they turn their backs to me, like kids trying to hide their school work. "You want one of these?" Liam asks Callum. He nods.

"Why not. It's one of my favorite positions." He raises his eyebrow and his eyes meet mine, then slowly drop lower until he's looked me up and down. I don't know how he does it but I feel like he just peeled away my dress and underwear with his eyes. Liam waves the barman over and I move to lean on the bar, hoping its proximity can protect me from whatever dark thoughts Callum seems to be conjuring.

Looking positively bored, the hotel employee drags himself to where we're standing and mumbles something that I assume was 'what would you like?' Liam grins over at me and then says in a very loud voice, "We'd all like a Long Screw Against a Wall."

I look at him aghast, then the barman smirks, "That'd be hard with three of you!"

"Not really," Callum says. "One behind, one in front. You'd be surprised how easy it can be."

The barman's mouth drops open. He obviously wasn't expecting that response. When he says nothing and turns to the back of the bar to begin our cocktails, Liam doubles over, attempting to laugh silently but failing abysmally.

"Oh my God," I mouth at Callum, shaking my head in general disbelief. "I think he was close to having an aneurism."

"What?" He shrugs his shoulders as though he doesn't get what all the fuss is about. It's then that I realize that he actually wasn't joking. To be so blasé it must be something that he's actually done. A threesome. With his brother?

My heart thuds in my chest. During the wedding service, I'd thought that my unexpectedly naughty thoughts about them were tightly in the realms of fantasy. Well, it seems they are for me, but not the twins. It sounds as though multiple love is a regular occurrence with them, and that thought has me squeezing my legs together.

Liam slumps down on a bar stool and pulls me towards him by the wrists. "So, Bethany. We have the drinks, now we need the music."

"It's gonna take more than one cocktail."

His eyes flash brightly. "One screw not enough?" he asks in a voice laced with pure, raw sex. My cheeks react like furnaces and I die a little inside at my total inability to remain cool in the presence of these gorgeous men. "Hey," he says, seeing my obvious mortification. "I'm just kidding around." He gently squeezes my wrists and I look down with a golf ball sized lump in my throat.

"It's got to be a Madonna track," he announces. "It's Dean and Kerry's wedding so we gotta stick to the theme. How about 'Vogue'!"

"Vogue?" I say, with all the exaggerated exasperation I can muster.

"What? She was the Goddess of the 80s."

"She might have been but that doesn't mean I want to Vogue at my sister's wedding!"

"Okay, you may have a point." Liam looks to the sky seeking inspiration, but Callum provides the next song choice. "Wham's 'Wake Me Up Before You Go Go'?"

"Ugh. Too cheesy."

"Billy Ocean, 'Caribbean Queen'?"

"Ooo...I like that one," I say enthusiastically and Callum looks euphoric. "But no. Too groovy."

"You're a hard girl to please!" Liam says with a fake grumpy face, and I have an urge to smooth out his frown and turn it upside-down.

"How about Duran Duran, 'Rio'?" I say.

"I like it…" he says after a few seconds, voice trailing and uncertain.

"What?" I ask, suddenly feeling like my suggestion was a terrible one. I want to paper over it so he's not displeased with me. "You suggest something else then," I say quickly. Liam is still holding my wrists, which should feel weird but is actually strangely comforting. His thumbs rest across the vulnerable inside skin, and he's looking down at my palms. Then his eyes flick up to mine and I realize he was feeling my pulse and he knew my heart was beating faster. He felt my embarrassment in his hands.

I pull away just as the barman turns, presenting three ridiculous looking cocktails. "Wow," I say, as he slides mine across the bar towards me, and I take a long pull at the straw, needing the relaxing effects of more alcohol just to calm my ridiculous social nerves. "Mmm, delicious."

Liam is quiet and I don't like it. I turn to find the twins looking at each other. They don't say anything, but it's as though they communicate something silently. They both sip at their drink a few times, and Callum passes his key card so the cost of our order can be added to his room charge.

"I think," he says, turning to me with serious eyes, "That your idea is perfect and very clever. You want to know why?"

"I do."

"I think you chose it because you think that the DJ won't have it."

I feel my heart sink in my chest. He thinks I'm a coward and that I'm trying to play their game and worm out of it at the same time.

"That's not why I chose it," I say quietly.

The twins don't say anything, just look at me until the need to fill the silence is overwhelming. They are big, strong men but they aren't arrogant. There's no real pressure here for me to explain myself, but I find that I want to. I want them to understand, even though it's hard. There's something about them. I can't put my finger on what it is, but in among the butterflies I permanently seem to have in my stomach when they're near, I feel a sense of understanding.

So I tell them. "It was playing on the radio when I left my ex-boyfriend. It…it made me smile when he sings that bit about Rio dancing on the sand. I did that when I was younger when I was on holiday with Kerry. We went down to the beach with some of the locals our age and they had an old ghetto blaster. We were so drunk and happy. It was like a sign, that I was doing the right thing…walking away".

There seems to be minutes of silent space between us, but it's really only seconds, then Callum reaches around my shoulders and side-hugs me, tucking my head against his chest.

"Drink up," he says. "I've got an idea that'll blow this game out of the water."

3

DANCING MY WAY TO HAPPINESS

The sand is slightly cold against my feet where the heat left by the afternoon sun has cooled under the moon. Liam takes hold of my hand, leading me across the wide expanse of beach until we're further from the hotel and closer to the sea. Callum walks beside me; close enough that I can smell his cologne and feel his presence almost as physically as if he was touching me. It's a perfect balmy evening and I'm so grateful to be away from that stupid dance floor and the pressure to blend in. Even though I've only known these men for a few hours, I feel calm and peaceful.

We get to a spot that's away from the spread of the hotel and they stop, dropping my shoes to the ground. Liam pulls out his phone and starts fiddling with it.

"What are you doing?" I ask, still puzzled by their sudden change of heart and the idea they seem so confident about.

"I'm looking for something. Have some patience, woman."

In the moonlight as they stand side by side, they look gorgeously ruffled and so tall I have to crane my neck to see the top of them. Callum watches his brother, smiling to himself, and then Liam looks up with a triumphant grin.

It's then that I realize why.

The song starts with a ridiculous scraping sound and then moves into a frantic synthesizer intro before Simon Le Bon belts out the first lines of Rio. Liam rests the phone down in one of my shoes and takes my hand, pulling me against him. I'm so shocked that I must feel like a plank of wood in his arms, but then as he sways us slowly back and forth, I start to melt. I don't want to be the uptight person I seem to keep morphing into. A flash of memory spins itself into my consciousness; Kerry's hair fanning out behind her and my arms in the air as we danced our hearts out all those years ago.

I'm buried against Liam's chest, swamped by the size of him, but I feel bigger than I have in so long. The alcohol is warm in my stomach, licking inside me to soften my hard edges. We dance for a little while before I feel another hand at my waist. With perfect synchronicity, Liam releases me into Callum's waiting arms. Physically they are the same arms but it feels different. Liam is light and humor and Callum is something a little darker and more daring. Either way, I'm having so much fun dancing with them that I smile against Callum's shoulder, nuzzling against his solidness. Then he grabs one of my hands and spins me out like a professional. I'm a puppet in his control, twirling with my hair coming loose and the skirt of my silk tea dress flaring like a lily's trumpet.

He doesn't have perfect rhythm and being so big he's a little heavy on his feet, but he smiles like he doesn't have a care in the world, watching me do the very thing I had imagined the day I left Brad. A cool breeze drifts across the beach, picking up loose tendrils of my hair until they whip over my face and I love it. I love it all.

Then he lets go of my hand.

There's a moment where I think that Liam is going to step in. Then, when I realize he's not going to, another second where I want to stop. I hear Brad's voice in my head telling me I can't do it, that I have two left feet and I'll embarrass myself. Then I see Callum and Liam with their heads tipped to the sky, dancing euphorically and I want that too.

I let myself go, raising my hands up like I used to, spinning with sand between my toes, swaying my hips, and starting to sing along.

I hear their voices join mine, perfectly out of tune and it's amazing. When the song comes to an end I look over at them grinning at me and I burst out laughing.

"You're something else, Bethany," Liam says with pride in his voice.

"Yeah, baby," Callum says in agreement, and I feel like I might burst with joy.

"You're something else, too," I say, instinctively taking their hands in mine and squeezing. There's a flash of something in their eyes as I look at them; a dark look of longing that I feel reflected in my heart. Before I know what's happening Liam has tugged me into a bear hug. I can't understand how I can feel so utterly content in the arms of a practical stranger. Then I feel Callum behind me, putting his hand on my waist and stroking my hair.

I feel the press of a kiss to the top of my head from behind, and Liam whispers into my left ear. "You remember something, Bethany. People might tell you things about yourself, but you choose to believe them.

You choose to let them change how you live your life. Anyone you meet who wants to change you is not someone you should be wasting time on, okay. You're perfect just being you. Remember that, okay."

Tears spring to my eyes and I squeeze him tightly with one arm, and cover Callum's hand with my other, wanting to convey how much it means to me that they're with me at this moment because I can't make the words come out of my mouth.

Liam tips my face to look up at his. "You decide how you want to live your life and the people you spend your time with. You choose, okay?"

"Okay."

He lets me go and I turn to Callum, who pulls me in for a hug too. "You know, I hate to say this, but my brother's right."

I hear a grumbling sound from behind me and laugh, and as I do, another little piece of me seems to fall into place. I've missed laughing so much. The genuine bubbling laughter that comes from a place rooted in your soul.

I sense them both turning to look back towards the hotel where two of the most important people in our lives have become a unit, and I feel as though they're going to suggest that we go back to the reception, but I don't want to. It's already so late, and anyway, I'm confident Kerry won't mind. She's happiest when the people she loves are happy.

"I don't want to go back yet," I say quietly.

Callum doesn't say anything but looks down at me with serious eyes. "What do you want to do then, Bethany?"

"Stay here, just us."

He nods and I go to pull back. "And do what?"

I blush, thinking about what it must sound like to them. What am I asking for? To hang out on the beach with two men who I suspect aren't strangers to sharing a girl. I feel hot between my legs thinking about what it would feel like to let them kiss me, to let them touch me in ways no one has since Brad. They're so much bigger that I can't help but imagine how far I would have to open my legs to wrap them around them. I think back to the picture Callum painted at the bar. One of them behind, one in front. What would that feel like to be so surrounded by big strong men? They wait for me to answer, but with all this sliding through my head like syrup, I just can't find the words.

"You remember what I told you, Bethany, about deciding. If you want something in life, you've got to learn to ask for it. No more hanging back, letting other people be in control," Liam says.

"I want to…" I trail off with so much heat in my cheeks it's a wonder I haven't fainted.

"Tell us what you want," Callum says in the lowest, sexiest voice I have ever heard. "Because I think we might just give you anything."

I turn to face the sea, and I feel their eyes on me, waiting. Hoping maybe. The weight of their words presses against my heart. I wonder when it was that my voice became so muted. When did it become okay for me to silence my own thoughts and feelings; my desires? When did I become ashamed of being the person that I am, enough that I'd conform to the version of me that someone else wanted?

For the first time in a long while, I don't feel sad about it. I feel angry. Angry that I lost myself for so long, and desperate to find myself again. These two men have found a way to free just a little bit of me. The girl that once danced on a beach without a care in the world. I felt her again, that me from the past and it's intoxicating. If I could just get back some more pieces, maybe the nagging emptiness I've been feeling so long will leave me for good.

I want that so badly that my heart hurts.

I take a few steps towards the sea and let the cool water slip between my toes. The sea whispers in front of me, stretched out like a never-ending pool of obsidian ink. Behind me stand two men who feel like the key to something. But do I have the courage to ask for what I want?

In a few days we're all going to leave this place; me back home and the twins back to Dubai. This time is like an interlude in my real life. A flash of time that stands away from reality. I could spend the rest of my time here plodding along, feeling the same, or I could be brave, and see if I'm right. If Liam and Callum, these men who I've been told are the best friends my brother-in-law could ever hope to have, could bring back some of the old me.

I turn slowly and find them standing like mirror images, hands in pockets, heads cocked to opposite sides. "I want...you to kiss me," I say, looking down so I don't have to see their reaction.

A gust of wind tugs my skirt closer around my legs and I can hear the rustling of their feet on the sand. Fingers lift my chin, holding my face gently. It's Callum and he smiles lazily as our eyes meet, leaning in to press his lips against mine. Our first kiss is so sweet, sweeter than I ever would have imagined Callum would be. It's a simple and soft hello that swells my heart, and the way he holds me gently, his big hands resting on my upper arms, has me melting. He moves against me so softly that when he pulls away I lean forward, following his mouth as it retreats.

Callum steps aside and Liam steps in, slipping his hand into my hair and drawing me towards him. His lips are hungrier, maybe because he already watched his brother do this exact same thing only seconds earlier. I can taste the cocktail on his lips and the passion in his grasp and I put my hand on his neck, drawing him closer. Then he too pulls back.

"What?" I say, not understanding why he's stopped in the middle of something so amazing. Wondering if this is how it's going to be, passed back and forth between them.

"What else, Bethany?"

The question takes me by surprise. "What do you mean what else? Why did you stop?"

"What else do you want? We need you to tell us so that we know that you're sure of everything. We want you to feel in control of what happens next. You get to choose, baby, just you." Liam strokes his palm over my hair, pushing back the wispy bits that are tickling my cheeks, but I can't look at him. I feel too raw, too seen, and it feels amazing and terrifying all in one big bundle.

How can a person go from being steered in life to taking the wheel? Brad had been emotionally manipulative, subtle in his cruelty, pick-pick-picking away until I looked down at myself and saw nothing but holes. It had been four months since I walked away, but the holes were still there, wind blowing through and taking my courage with it.

It seemed that Liam and Callum could see the holes too and that was mortifying. That they wanted to help me fill them in with myself again was too glorious to comprehend. Dean had said his best men were the truest friends anyone could ever have and I thought he was waxing lyrical. Now I see exactly what my brother-in-law was talking about.

"Bethany…" Callum says, caressing my cheeks. "If you can't tell us, show us, baby. Show us what you need and we'll give it to you. We'll give it all to you."

My breath catches in my throat and a tear slips past my restraint. Before I have a chance to swipe it away, Callum kisses me where it fell. It's that simple gesture that gives me resolve. "I want you," I say, taking each of their hands in mine. "I want everything."

Liam strokes my hair gently, as though I'm something precious and fragile, and then he says, "Then that's exactly what we'll give you."

4
FINDING PARADISE

Liam and Callum had been right about me earlier that night. I'm not a 'sex on the beach' kind of girl. It's too messy, with far too much risk of sand abrasion in unfortunate places. I wasn't averse to being carried to their hotel room, though, while they sang what had become 'our tune'. It's probably the alcohol that has made me feel so loose-limbed and unconcerned about what the world might think. I guess to an outsider we would look like friends enjoying a silly time while on vacation. I suspect that the truth would be far from the mind of the average person.

The resort is quiet, but when we pass Kerry and Dean's suite we can hear giggling and I am so unbelievably happy for them.

When Callum reaches his door, he rests me down and kisses me on the mouth. As he makes quick work of the lock Liam presses his lips against my neck, only drawing back as Callum pulls me into the room. Liam follows closely, carrying my shoes and purse. There's a moment when the door clicks into place and the room darkens that my heart skitters in my chest. In bare feet, the twins loom large, eyelids lowered and eyes dark with desire. The air crackles with energy: the buzz that comes with anticipation, the discovery of a new lover and the pleasure that will come with it. I wait because I've given them the green-light to everything and the look in their eyes says they are going to take it. I'm buzzing just thinking about what we're going to do, and so damn happy I'm finally in a place to draw some kind of line across Brad and his aftereffects.

And what a line it's going to be.

Callum is the first to pull his tie away from his shirt collar, watching me closely. Liam isn't far behind. There are little buttons down the front of my dress; covered ones that are fiddly to do up but easy to undo. As I flip them open one by one, their burning gazes follow the path of my fingers. There is a silk belt tie at the waist and I draw it apart, not slowly but not too fast either. When I slip the soft fabric of the dress from my shoulders, I'm left standing in just my lacy cream bra and panties, and the pearl-decorated garter that matched Kerry's. The twins step close enough that I can feel the heat and coiled passion rolling off them in waves. My head is level with Liam's broad chest, and I breathe him in; the warm scent of his cologne and the unique scent of his skin making me lightheaded. Callum moves behind me, sweeping my hair aside so that it hangs over one shoulder before he kisses my neck softly. I find myself leaning into him, gasping as his hands rest on my hips and grip.

Liam bends to kiss me, a soft slide of his lips over mine, a gentle tug as he pulls my bottom lip between his, the rumble of a groan as I hook my hand around his neck and pull him toward me. I open my mouth, wanting his taste and the slide of his tongue over mine. With it comes the delicious clenching feeling I get between my legs when his hands clasp my bottom and squeeze.

My own hands are antsy, reaching to undo the buttons on Liam's shirt, wanting to see the impressive body I've imagined underneath his clothes and feel the heat of his skin against my palms. He pulls back and tugs the sleeves off quickly, standing before me, his chest rising and falling, eyes burning as he begins to undo his gray trousers too slowly.

"Watch him," Callum orders directly into my ear. The heat of his breath sends shivers spreading up my neck. His hands slide up my ribs and over my breasts, squeezing gently then seeking out the front fastening. As Liam steps out of his trousers, Callum undoes the clasp, slipping the straps from my shoulders.

Brad had always hinted that my breasts were too small and spent time pointing out women in magazines with more impressive proportions. The way Liam looks at me wipes all that away. There's a moment where he hesitates to touch me, his hand hovering in the air as though he's enjoying the anticipation and imagining what I'll feel like in his palm. His first caress is gentle, and when his thumb merely grazes my nipple, I feel it pucker, seeking more contact.

"So beautiful," he says, thumb passing back over the tip of my nipple again and again, his eyes fixed on mine. I want to tell him to squeeze, to take it between his fingers and pinch it. Callum's hand snakes around from behind and does the very thing I'm craving to my other breast. The contrast is electric.

"Oh," I gasp, leaning into Callum again.

"She likes that," Liam says, meeting the eyes of his brother.

"Soft and hard?" Callum responds.

"Yeah."

I want to tell them that I'm pretty much guaranteed to like whatever they do to me, but my mouth is firmly clamped shut as they continue alternating.

As much as I'm enjoying everything, I need more. I need to feel their skin under my hands so I allow them to wander, palms skittering as they slide up Liam's sides, over ribs packed with muscle, then across nicely rounded pectorals until my thumb gently brushes his nipple. Liam hisses and takes hold of my hand, pushing it against his cock. And what a cock it is. For a moment I think I must be confused. Surely this can't be real. But as I explore, allowing my hand to wander, I realize that it is. My pussy clenches now that it knows what's coming. I feel a little overwhelmed because these boys are identical so I pretty much know what Callum's packing behind me is a mirror image. I'm hungry to see it, to know what his body is like in all its natural glory. When I move my hand to touch the waistband of Liam's Calvins he gets the hint and drops them.

Damn.

I stare open mouthed at the cock Liam's revealed. He takes hold of it at the root and squeezes and I swear I almost come at the sight of him alone. It looks like he's wielding a weapon but fuck, he could club me to death with that thing anytime. I want to laugh because, in comparison, Brad's cock was a wiener. No wonder our sex life was so dry. I bet Liam's never had bad sex in his life.

"You're looking at my cock like…I don't know what," he says smirking.

"Maybe she's never seen a cock that big," Callum mouths against my ear. "You wanna touch it, Bethany? Make sure it's real?"

Liam grins and winks, moving closer and taking my hand. "He doesn't bite," he says as he wraps my palm around the base. My fingers don't meet it's so wide, and the heat of him, the pulsing firmness. The sense of anticipation that he's gonna fuck me with this massive thing soon has my pussy clenching as heat spreads between my legs.

"See," Callum whispers. "His curves slightly to the right and mine curves slightly to the left. That's the other way you can tell us apart."

"But we want to drive you so crazy that you don't even care which one of us is fucking you," Liam says, watching my hand slide up and down his length.

Behind me, Callum strokes his hands down my waist and over my ass, squeezing. Then I hear the rustle of fabric as he sheds his clothes too. Liam takes hold of my wrist and urges me to let him go. I groan with disappointment, but when he drops to his knees in front of me, I moan for another reason. He kisses my thighs, his fingers skirting around the lacy edge of my panties, teasing. He presses a kiss directly over my clit through the fabric and I change my stance to open my legs wider.

"You smell so good," he says, inhaling deeply. "So fucking sexy."

There's always a moment when I'm with a new lover and they're heading between my legs that I feel nervous. Brad never wanted to go down on me. He never came right out and said why but his reluctance made me feel self-conscious. Liam's reassurances have my body singing and my nerves disappearing.

"Lick her," Callum says. "Make her wet for me."

Liam wastes no time, pushing my panties aside and using his tongue to part my labia. I push my hips forward, giving him more room and boy, does he use it. His thumbs spread me open then the tip of his tongue teases my clit. "Oh," I say as my legs start to tremble.

"Watch him," Callum says. "Look at the way he's worshiping you, baby."

I open my tightly closed eyes and look down as Liam. His gaze fixes on mine as he flicks my clit with rapid licks of his tongue. It looks so damn dirty and explicit and I know I'm blushing. Then he winks at me, and I'm so close to coming I almost fall.

Liam pulls back, gripping me around my leg with one arm and using the other hand to test how wet I am. Fuck. The way his fingers slide around my opening tells him everything he needs to know. "She's ready," he tells his brother.

Then Callum's there in front of me, backing me towards the wall, his condom-clad cock held firmly in his hand. "I've been imagining fucking you against the wall since we chose those cocktails," he says. I don't tell him I've been imagining the same thing because my mouth is so damn dry and my brain doesn't seem to be able to process thoughts into words right now. "Take your panties off," he orders.

I push them off my thighs and wriggle out of them until they hit the floor. Then Callum's there, lifting my right leg over his forearm and angling his cock to slide between my labia. "My brother made you so wet," he says, nibbling on my bottom lip. Oh, that sounds so damn wrong but it feels so damn right. His cock notches at my entrance and he pauses looking right into my eyes, so close I can see the fan of blue and amber that spread outward from his pupils. He blinks slowly, pushing just a little bit. "You want this, baby?" he asks.

I nod because as much as what we're doing together is fucking crazy and so outside my realms of previous experience it is almost laughable, I'm ready. As ready as I have ever been for anything in my whole sheltered life.

"That's my girl," he says, and with one strong thrust of his hips, he's deep inside me. "Fuck," he grunts. "So damn tight."

"Oh," I gasp as he pulls out and then pushes back inside even deeper. He's so big I can barely move.

Liam comes closer. "Put your hands above your head, Bethany," he murmurs. God, the thought of being held by one man while another man fucks me is too much, but I do as he asks and he takes hold of my wrists to holds me captive. "Does it feel good?" he asks.

"Yes."

Callum grinds deeper, using his free hand to cup my breast and pinch my nipple. His touch is harsh, my nipple stinging momentarily, but I love it. Who knew there was such a strong connection between my nipples and my clit, one that only pain can activate. He thrusts deep and hard, squashing me against the cool wall. My pussy aches to come. All the sensations make my clit burn with sensitivity.

Liam's hold on my wrists is tight, his brow furrowed as though he's finding it hard to hold himself back. I can't imagine how frustrating it must feel to be so close to being able to fuck, but having to wait his turn. The thought of Callum pulling out and Liam replacing him is so naughty that I groan, bucking my hips to show Callum I want more. I want him to fuck me so hard I can feel it for days after. I want to remember this night for years to come. Remember the girl I am tonight: reckless, wanton, sexy and free. So unlike the me I've been since Brad.

Callum pumps me so hard that the foot that I was standing on rises off the ground and I'm suspended by his strong body. Liam lets me go to put on a condom, and I notice his hands tremble a little as he rolls it downwards. To see that he's as frantic as I'm feeling makes my heart ache. Who are these men who have managed to pull me out of my funk and turn me inside out? So strong but sensitive too, the way real men should be.

Callum sees me watching his brother and slows. "You want Liam?" he asks. I look at him, trying to work out if there is any jealousy or resentment there, but there's nothing. He's smiling at me, perfect teeth glinting in the low light. I kiss his lips to let him know that I'm with him, and he grinds against me more slowly. "Go get him," he says, swatting me on the ass as he pulls out. I'm left shaky legged and a little embarrassed, but Liam doesn't leave me standing.

He's there in seconds, grabbing me under the thighs, lifting me in the air as if I weigh nothing. I feel like a doll in his arms, totally at his behest, but also powerful. The sounds he makes as he kisses and licks my neck, walking me over to the bed are needy. Greedy. His cock is rock hard between my legs, ready to push its way inside me. The thought makes me frantic. Desperate hands tug at his hair as my lips seek the warmth of his mouth.

Liam's kiss isn't chaste as he lays me down on the bed and rests his weight on top of me, pushing his hips to rub his cock against my throbbing clit. His tongue caresses mine in the rhythm of his hips until I'm mindless; clawing at his back, my leg hooking over his thigh to force him to push harder.

His hand moves to grasp my breast, thumb seeking the hardness of my nipple and pressing down. We moan at the same time, but it isn't enough. I want heat and sweat. His hand is huge, cupping all my pale flesh with my nipple poking through his fingers. He pinches, gently to start, then when I moan he looks at me questioningly.

"Everything?" Liam asks. "If you want it all, you've got to tell us what you like."

There he is again, pushing me, picking at my edges to peek underneath. Part of me hates it but a bigger part tells me to stop being stupid. Isn't this what I wanted? To be cared about enough that what I wanted was what they sought to deliver.

Isn't that what we all seek?

Understanding.

Consideration.

Appreciation.

Callum and Liam seem to have it all in spades.

"Ask me questions," I say, quietly. "I'm not good at this."

He kisses me so gently then, as though I was a delicate flower he wanted to see open and show its beauty to the world.

"Do you like it when I pinch you?" I nod and he grins. "Harder?" Another nod and a dirty smile. "Do you want me to lick you again?" This time my nod is accompanied by wide eyes and a tomato shade blush, which he runs his fingers over. "Sweet Bethany. I love the way you taste. I want to see your pretty pussy and feel it on my tongue." He licks the soft underside of my top lip as if to demonstrate and I taste the sweetness of the cocktail on him.

"What else?" I whisper.

"You tell me, baby! You like it long and slow or hard and fast?" When he smiles it's lazy and the dimple on his left cheek suddenly appears, giving him a devilish schoolboy look.

"Both!" I say, with a bit too much enthusiasm.

"What the lady wants, the lady will get." He rises up on his forearms, arms bulging as they take all his weight and then pushes backward so he's kneeling between my legs. Liam's finger caresses my clit, slipping down between my legs to gather more of my arousal. He seems transfixed by it, his head cocked to the side, eyes fully focused on the slow back and forth action. My thighs tremble at the sensation, and I have to slide my feet up the bed to stop my hips from rising up. "You have such soft skin and amazing legs. I've been looking at them all day. Your ankles and these strong calves. Those killer shoes." Liam laughs quietly. "I kept thinking about your thighs. What they would be like. What it would feel like to get between them."

"Me too," Callum says from his place at the edge of the bed. He crawls closer so he can stroke his hand over my hardened nipples.

"Well, here you both are. So, what does it feel like?" I ask softly.

Liam shakes his head as if words aren't enough. "Can I tell you later? When I slide myself in here?" His finger moves from my thigh to press against my entrance, two fingers at least pushing inside. He groans and everything in me stills except my frantic heart. I can't breathe as he teases with tiny movements, fingers slick with my arousal. I want him to just push inside me, to take me apart physically in the way his brother had, but he doesn't. Instead, he moves to ease my legs apart, holding them spread, pressing me open with his weight. The cool air-conditioned air licks at my wetness, making my clit tighten and pulse, but all Liam does is look.

"You're so pretty," he says, "so lovely." Then he bends his head to lick a long stripe between my parted lips and I almost come from that one motion. His tongue is hot and rough, a perfect counterpoint to the cool air. Using the very tip, he nudges against my swollen clit, slipping against it over and over until I can't keep my legs from coming up to hug against his head. "That's it," he says as Callum bends to kiss my mouth and swallow my moans. When I push my hips up off the bed, Liam says, "Take what you want, Bethany. Anything you want."

"Oh god," I say, chasing, chasing but not quite getting there. "I need…more, more."

And I know he has what it takes. I may not have felt Liam's cock inside me, but as it's almost identical to Callum's, I know what it's going to feel like when he pushes it in.

Big. Bigger than I've ever had before the twins.

Hard.

Hot.

Dominating.

There is something about a man who is well endowed that just makes me weak. I can't be alone in this. I've read way too many erotic novels to doubt that. Nothing makes a woman feel owned more than getting spread wide by a big dick, pinned in place by a strong man and fucked until her head feels like it's gonna explode.

While I'm thinking about Callum and Liam's massive cocks, all it takes is the press of Liam's two thick fingers, his tongue licking, licking, licking at my clit, then a twist of his fingers as he thrusts them in to the knuckle. I come with such a blinding flash that everything in me goes rigid; back bowed off the bed, toes curled, hands in fists as I ride the most cathartic orgasm of my life.

I want to shout "Fuck you, Brad!" at the top of my lungs, but settle for saying it in my head. Then I reach down to pull Liam on top of me, holding him so tightly around his middle he gasps and then chuckles. "That good, huh?"

"Oh yeah," I whisper, pressing my open mouth against his skin and tasting the salty sweetness of him.

Liam laughs warmly and grins at me happily. I kiss his dimple and the corner of his mouth, the tip of his nose and his shoulder.

"Where did you guys come from?" I ask, with so much awe in my voice that the sound of it makes me want to cry.

"I think it's called Dubai," Liam laughs.

"Men are from Mars," Callum says, taking hold of my hand and kissing it.

I trace my finger over Liam's eyebrow and the tiny scar he has above, filing all the little details that make him to memory.

He kisses my mouth, soft at first, then long, slow and deep. I can feel how ready he is, the hard press of his cock nestled in the groove between my leg and hip, nudging with every slide of his tongue. I run my fingers down his spine, the indentation between the muscles of his shoulders deep and strong, and then dig my fingers into his ass to let him know I'm ready too.

Liam's hands trace my body, sometimes hard, sometimes soft. Always reverential.

"Can I make a request?" Liam asks.

"Of course," I say, fascinated.

"I want you on top, Bethany. I want to see you take control. I want to watch you take what you want from me." The way he says it, smooth and feather soft and the way his eyes stroke over my face make my heart hurt. I know he's doing this for me, to give me the reigns to what happens next. But maybe a bit for him too, so that he's sure I'm fully present and in it for the right reasons.

"Okay," I say and watch as he moves to sit against the headboard, his body so big and strong and good.

I crawl towards him until I'm straddling his lap, legs spread so wide I feel a twinge in my hips. So this is what it feels like to have him between my thighs.

"That's it," Liam says, pulling me by the hips and raising me up over his cock, hauling me forward so he can lick and suck my nipples. "Put me inside you, Bethany. I want to feel you."

I reach between my legs to hold onto his cock, stroking it against my clit, watching it probe me in the most explicit way, then I push it towards my hole and rest back just enough for him to slide inside an inch. Liam's cock is so big and hard, and I'm so swollen from wanting it that it all feels too much. I rock back and forth, trying to open myself enough to slip down but it isn't happening, even though Callum has already opened me up. I must show my frustration on my face because Liam tips my chin and tells me to relax, and kisses me sweetly to help me do just that. Using one of his hands to hold my hip tightly, he pushes himself up and me down. Another hand joins Liam's from behind, and with both twins focused on the job, I'm suddenly full. When we're bone to bone I flop against Liam, the sensations too much, but he helps me, starting us in a slow rhythm that I eventually begin to lead. He feels so good inside me, big enough to stretch but not to hurt, and the way he pulls me against his body gives my clit enough contact to feel the possibility of another orgasm rising inside me.

Callum's hands move to my breasts, kneading them gently and pinching my nipples in time to my movements. His hands slide around my hips and over my ass, squeezing with just enough bite to hurt. Then his fingers stroke between the cheeks of my ass. I seize for a moment but Liam pulls at my hips, urging me to keep a rhythm. I'm not sure if I like what Callum's doing. Nobody's ever touched me there before and it feels so dirty. So forbidden. And so good. Oh god. I shouldn't like it when he presses what I think is his thumb against my taint. He flexes, pushing on and off like the beat of a heart. He follows the movement of my hips, never letting me escape his filthy attention. And I find that I don't want to escape. I just want to fuck and fuck and fuck and come and come and come until I don't know where I am or where I'm going. Until I don't care what is up and what is down.

There is so much heat between us; sweat on my upper lip and glistening above Liam's collar bones, sweat in the dip at my lower back. Liam's lips are demanding now, tongue exploring until I feel lost in the pull and push that is everywhere our bodies are connected. My orgasm sneaks up on me, rolling up as a fast swell as Callum works harder and breaches the tight ring of muscle he's been pushing against. Liam clutches my ass and squeezes as I arch my back and cry out. "That's it, that's it," he whispers in hot gusts against my neck.

I come with a high-pitched moan and Liam follows with a growl, everything pulsing and fluttering between us. He holds himself so still as if all his muscles have seized from an overload of pleasure.

Callum waits, stroking my curves, kissing my hair until I've recovered enough to turn. His cock is so hard, and as blissed out as I am, I want to feel him come inside me too.

I kiss his mouth, cupping his balls in my hand and rolling them, marveling at how heavy they are in my palm. He doesn't give me much chance to play though before he has me on my back, cock surging inside me so hard it knocks the breath from my lungs.

"Fuck, you feel so fucking good," he gasps, hooking my legs over his shoulders to make the penetration deeper. I ache deep inside from where he's hammering my cervix but I don't stop him. The desperation on his face is stark; deep lines etched between his brows and eyes clenched tight as he chases release. I'm not expecting to come again but the power behind his hips is enough to make my pussy spasm. Fuck. I grip the sheets, body totally out of control now. Callum growls, his chest lowering on top of mine so that he can bury his face in my neck. I slip my fingers into his hair, and grip his ass, driving him faster against me. "Baby," he gasps and I know he's nearly there.

"That's it," I say. "That's it, baby. Let it all go. Gimme everything."

He pounds into me four more times and then seizes, cock swelling deep inside me as he comes. For a moment, I wish he wasn't wearing a condom. As reckless as that would be, I've always wanted to know what it would feel like for a man to come inside me. There's something so raw and primal about the concept of being marked by semen, of feeling it leaking out and knowing that they were there and left something behind.

I don't get to feel that this time, though, but what happens next is even better.

I didn't put any thought into what it might be like after the sex. At the beach, all I could think about was allowing myself to give into my desires without guilt. Now I'm here, lying between the best men while my sister enjoys her own wedding night and suddenly I feel less certain.

It's not that I'm having regrets. I just had the best sex of my life. But how does a girl deal with this part? Are they expecting me to get up and say goodbye? I'm not experienced at casual sex, although to be honest, this didn't feel very casual. I go to sit up but Callum grabs me and pulls me toward him until I'm sprawled half over his chest. I feel the bed shift behind me and then Liam's there, spooning me from behind, his hands running over my ass and hip lazily.

"Damn," Callum says after a few minutes.

"Damn," Liam whispers.

Callum tips my chin until I'm looking right into his beautiful eyes. "You were…"

"…something else," Liam finishes.

I reach behind and take hold of his hand while Callum kisses my lips gently.

"I feel like someone else," I say.

"Who?" they ask at the same time.

"Me," I say.

We're silent for a while but it feels okay. There is not a single moment when they're not making me feel totally worshiped. It's only after my heart has slowed and my sweat has cooled that I realize I haven't felt this happy in years. And when Callum's fingers dip between my legs again, I know I'm about to get even happier.

5
MORNING GLORY

I wake feeling completely foggy; brain slow and eyes practically stuck together. For a moment I think I'm at home, then I register that I'm not wearing anything and there is the weight of an arm over my middle, and suddenly I realize where I am.

I freeze, listening to the soft breathing sounds on either side of me. They are slow and regular so I'm guessing that Callum and Liam are still sleeping. I risk a peek to my left and see that it's Liam who has his arm resting on me. The little scar on his forehead is the only way I can tell, and I take a moment to study him. There's an innocence about him that disappears as soon as those piercing gray eyes are on show. Long lashes cast shadows over his cheekbones, and his lips look so pink and full that mine tingle with the urge to kiss him. The things that mouth did to me last night. Just thinking about it makes me blush, and there's plenty of blood pulsing between my legs too. I'm sore but I wouldn't care if they wanted to start over at the beginning and give me a full repeat performance. In fact, I'm tempted to reach down and see if I can get things started up. I turn to the other side and find Callum with his eyes open, watching me and looking highly amused.

"What is it, baby," he asks softly. "Forget where you were?"

"I guess."

"But you're not having regrets, are you?"

His face is serious and I wonder how many times they've done this and found the girl has been upset in the morning. There is no way I want him thinking that. I mean, this is so far out of my previous realms of experience that it's almost laughable. The twins just about shattered my mind into infinitesimal pieces last night. It's hard to think about how I feel, wrapped up in the arms of one of them and with the gorgeous eyes of the other fixed right on mine.

I shake my head because any nagging doubts that I might be having are staying firmly in my mind. It's the morning after, and regrets aren't something to share.

"That's good," he whispers, pushing a strand of my hair from my cheek and tucking it behind my ear. "Pleasure like that has to be fucking celebrated…marveled at…repeated." His eyes glint with mischief and I notice for the first time that he also gets a little dimple on his left cheek when he's being naughty. He runs a thumb over my bottom lip, watching intently as my mouth parts and his thumb slips slightly inside. I sigh because there is something so unbelievably erotic about that action; penetration almost as good as his dick between my legs.

He takes my hand and presses it around his heavy erect cock and I'm suddenly back to last night and the moment I realized how huge they both were. I'm back to the first moment that Callum pushed inside me. Delicious pleasure-pain that had me raising my hips to urge him deeper.

"That feels good," he says, a husky edge to his voice that wasn't there before.

I stroke the full length of him slowly, relishing the velvety feeling of his skin and the solidity of the flesh underneath. I look at my hand, so small and pale in comparison to his darker flesh. The power in his cock and thighs contrast against the sensitivity in this part of him. The angle is difficult so I move to turn, sliding underneath Liam's arm. My movements stir him and I feel him moving closer to me, his equally erect cock nudging between my legs.

"You guys getting started without me?" he grumbles, his voice still thick with sleep.

"You snooze, you lose!" Callum says and Liam snorts.

"I'm fucking wrecked!" he groans.

"Ah, you finally found a girl who got the better of you," Callum laughs.

"She didn't get the better of me." Liam's hand slips up from my belly to cup my breast and roll my nipple. He pushes his hips, nudging my ass, cock slipping in the wetness between my thighs.

It's weird to be discussed like I'm not even present, but also quite amusing. I like seeing the boys like this. It's how I always imagined twins would be. Winding each other up in a good-natured way.

"Yeah, well you missed your workout this morning," Callum says.

Liam nuzzles my neck, inhaling deeply against my skin. "Gonna make up for that about now, if Rio is willing."

I love the little nickname they've given me. It feels intimate and personal; a term of endearment that I wouldn't have expected.

"Rio feels pretty willing to me," Callum says with a groan. My palm is getting slick from his arousal and I know Liam's cock is slick from mine. It feels so naughty to have a man's bare cock against my pussy. My pussy clenches and I feel Liam's smile against my shoulder.

"Kitty getting hungry?" he asks.

I nod because my mouth is so dry. I could guzzle a whole bottle of cool spring water right now, but there is no way I'm interrupting the moment.

Callum reaches beneath his pillow and tosses his brother a shiny square. Liam makes short work of the wrapper with his teeth and then he's pulling back, the distinctive sounds of latex rolling down cock the only noise apart from our breathing.

He takes my hair in a rough ponytail and grips it firmly. Callum kindly assists by lifting my top leg and holding it to ease his brother's entrance. The first nudge of Liam's cock inside me burns, but he takes it slowly, pushing me open until he slips in through the slickness of my cunt.

Oh, how amazing it feels. Let me count the ways.

Big. Hard. A little rough. And so dirty when Callum slips his finger into my mouth and then presses it against my clit. He kisses me; an open-mouthed passionate kiss, a meeting of tongues and lips that feels different. Guys I've been with before struggle to kiss well and fuck at the same time. But here Callum isn't doing the fucking. His brother is. Callum gets to seduce my mouth, stroke my clit while I get him so hot his hips are bucking into my fist.

I moan into his mouth because DAMN! A woman can only be expected to take so much pleasure in silence.

"Yeah," Liam groans from behind, pulling my hair so I have to arch my back. I stare into Callum's eyes, watching as his glaze from pleasure.

"You okay?" he asks me, surprising me with his consideration.

"Yeah," I say. "Oh…" I'm suddenly empty because Liam has pulled out.

"Stand up," Liam orders, "Both of you."

My legs tremble as I do what he's asked, Callum swinging his legs off the edge of the bed. Liam takes up position sitting on the edge and pulls me backward by the hips until I'm sitting in his lap, impaled on his huge cock. His hands span my waist, pushing me to lean forward.

"Rest your hands on your knees," he says.

"Bossy," I tell him, but I do as he asks. It's so sexy that he knows what he wants. Liam seems to have this whole thing choreographed.

"Smart mouth," he replies and I can hear the smile in his voice. "Now put that smart mouth to work, baby. Make my brother come."

Callum moves to stand in front of me, cock held tightly in his fist. I know what it's gonna feel like to suck him. I can guess what he's gonna taste like; not too dissimilar to his brother, I would have thought. He's different, though. As he comes closer he cups my cheek, stroking my skin and looking at me tenderly. He pushes my hair behind my ears and bends down to kiss my lips. There's something so gentle behind his actions, a stark contrast to the fierce grip that Liam has and the way he's grinding into me from behind. It's as though they've switched roles and that has me intrigued.

"You gonna suck me?" Callum asks, his thumb trailing my bottom lips, teasing.

I nod, because how could I turn him down. Even if he didn't look like a Greek god, his character has me like putty in his hands. He moves closer and I lean in. Then Liam is pushing me toward his brother, his grip on the back of my neck controlling me like a puppet. I know Callum is close because his cock seems to swell in my mouth as I take him as deeply as I can.

Liam forces my hips up and down, using me for his pleasure. I'm feeling swollen and about as horny as I ever have before. It's as though last night primed me for this…for the rawness and overwhelming feeling of being owned. It isn't something I ever thought I would like. It isn't something that I ever thought I would want. I thought that after Brad I'd never want to feel powerless again.

But this is different.

This is control with respect.

This is dominance with tenderness and concern.

This is me taking back control for myself. Control of what I want. Control to allow myself the freedom to seek my own pleasure and give in to my own cravings and desires.

In all their actions I can feel that they have me in mind. Even Liam, with his bossiness, must be able to feel how turned on it makes me.

As I take Callum deep and Liam slips his finger around my hips to rest on my clit I know that it isn't going to be long. They're going to make me come in a way that is almost scary. Scary because they seem to know just what I need to tip over the edge, when some of my exes never fathomed it during months of relationship. Scary because

I can feel that they're both close too and imagining the feeling of them reaching the precipice at the same time as me…well, I don't know how I'll be able to take it all. Liam's fingers grip my hip even tighter, his thrusts becoming harder and higher. Callum's hands are in my hair, holding me gently but proprietorially and I stare up into his eyes, taking in the strain on his face and the flush across his cheekbones.

"That's it," he says at the exact same time as his brother.

"That's it," Liam repeats by himself.

"Mmmm…" I groan as the stimulation becomes too much. I can feel my orgasm building too quickly, surging up from my belly through my spine. All I need is a little something else. Something else to bring all the sensations together.

"I see you're having fun without us," a voice says from the veranda doors.

Liam slams into me, groaning like he's dying, his cock swelling and swelling. Callum's eyes are fixed over my head, wide and unamused as he comes too, letting everything go into my mouth.

There's someone behind me, watching this scene, and the thought of that is enough to make me come. My pussy bears down so hard that Liam groans again, holding me tight against him, pulling me closer with his arms around my middle. I can't breathe. Tiny lights like fireflies dance before my eyes. Callum pulls out, cupping his dick and striding around the bed.

"What the fuck?" he says. "You never heard of knocking on the door?"

"What?" the voice says. "We can't drop in to surprise our big brothers?"

I turn, now as intrigued as I am mortified, and find myself gazing at another set of identical twins; gray eyes, dark hair and grins that say they are more than a little comfortable with coming across their brothers engaged in a threesome. Oh my god. Two sets of twins. What are the odds of that? I turn away quickly, sheltering in Liam's embrace. He tugs a sheet up and wraps it around me. I'm grateful to not be naked but I'm pretty pissed that two strangers just witnessed me having the most intense orgasm of my life. I don't even know where to put myself. Should I stand and say hello, or just shuffle off to the bathroom?

"I'm sorry," Liam whispers in my ear. "My kid brothers have no manners." I nod because I want him to know I'm not mad at him. "Go wash up," he says gently.

I stand and for a moment, contemplate the easy way out. The shuffle would be the route the old me would have taken. Hide away, blushing and mortified. Book an early flight home and spend the rest of my life recalling this moment and dying of shame.

I don't want to be the old me.

I turn, grasping the sheet above my breasts and look at the new arrivals properly. They study me with interest, probably because I have terrible bed head and a just-been-fucked glaze to my eyes.

"Well, this is a little embarrassing," I say, smiling.

"Nothing we haven't done before," the one on the right says. When he grins, he sports two deep dimples and the wickedest smile I've ever seen.

"Maybe not the point I was trying to make," I say.

The one on the left has the sense to look a little sheepish. "Sorry, doll," he says. "We were planning to surprise Callum and Liam and stumbled in on a little more action than we thought they'd have gotten after only twenty-four hours on this island."

"I don't know whether to be insulted or pissed off at that statement," Liam says, standing next to me with his condom-covered cock in full view of everyone.

"Jesus, dude," Callum says. "You wanna deal with that?"

"Well, if these two reprobates wanna fuck off, I can."

"Nice, bro," the one on the right says.

"You not going to introduce us?" the one on the left says.

"Go check into your own room," Liam barks. "Then meet us for breakfast and I'm sure you'll get first-name acquainted."

"Fair enough," the one on the right replies, winking at me. No shame.

Callum starts walking towards them and they back toward the doors to the veranda. Ground floor rooms definitely have some drawbacks. "Off you go then," he says.

"See you at breakfast, beautiful," someone calls.

Liam glances at me with a raised eyebrow. "Hell," he says.

"What?" I ask, frowning.

"I think you have two more admirers, baby."

6

BED AND BREAKFAST

I shower while Liam and Callum do whatever it is they do. When I'm done I put on my wedding clothes and cringe at the walk of shame I'm about to do across the hotel. My hair is wet and my skin scrubbed clean of make-up. When I study myself in the mirror I'm momentarily shocked at just how alive I look. There is pink on my cheeks and light in my eyes that hasn't been there for a long time.

I can't believe that all it took was some good sex to bring those things back. But I am grateful. Seriously grateful.

When I step through the bathroom door I find one of the twins sitting with a cup of coffee and the other channel surfing on the bed. I can't tell who is who until Liam speaks, waving the remote.

"You sure scrub up good," he says. "Makes me want to come over and dirty you up all over again."

I raise my hands in protest. "I think you've dirtied me up plenty in the last twelve hours!"

Callum chuckles. "Stop trying to pretend you were an innocent participant. You dirtied us up plenty too."

I blush, feeling a little proud of myself if that's what he thinks. "I should go."

"Mmm…" Liam says, narrowing his eyes. "Is this your attempt at a goodbye?"

"It's the 'thanks for last night' speech, isn't it?" Callum says.

I shake my head. That wasn't what I'd intended. I'm not really sure what I was intending. I'm here for five more days and I hadn't even gotten around to asking how long the twins are staying. Please let them be staying five more days too.

"So if it's not goodbye and thanks, what is it then?" They both look at me, gray eyes narrowed slightly as though they're hoping to read between my lines.

"I was gonna say 'see you at breakfast', but if you want to get rid of me…"

I take a step back and they are both up and off the bed. "You stay right where you are, little Rio," Liam says. His hand cuffs one of my wrists and he pulls me in for a searing kiss. Callum takes his place behind me and kisses my neck, stroking his big hand over my ass. I'm wet in a second, but I need to get out of here. The longer I wait, the greater the chance I'm gonna bump into mom or cousin Dylan on the way to my room.

I push against Liam's chest and when I've managed to get him to take a step back, I turn and do the same to

Callum. The twins are panting, chests rising and falling and eyes shining in a way that is utterly sexual. "I need to go. But I'll see you in the breakfast room in thirty minutes?"

They both groan as though I'm the worst kind of tease, and I grin.

"You can save those for later," I say, looking down at their erections pertinently.

"They're all yours, baby," Callum says, following me to the door. "You got everything?"

I look down at my purse and the shoes I'm holding because I can't face forcing my bruised feet into them. "I think so."

"Well, good luck," he says, opening the door.

I wave and then start down the corridor like an elderly power-walker. My room is five minutes away. It's not too far. There are plenty of wedding guests staying here but I'm hoping that most of them will still be asleep. The families are likely to have headed down to breakfast already. I cross my fingers, saying a silent prayer that I make it to the safety of my room without being outed as the wanton woman that I am. I'm almost there when I see a door opening and, horror of horrors, my mom backing her way out of a room.

I could have sworn her room was further down towards the beach than mine. Whose room was she in this early in the morning? She must catch sight of me from the corner of her eye because she whirls around and stops dead.

"Bethany," she gasps. "What are you doing here?"

I narrow my eyes because she's acting like I just caught her eating pie in the middle of the night. "I'm here for Kerry's wedding."

She huffs. Facetiousness is a pet peeve of hers. "That is not what I meant and you know it."

I shrug, feigning innocence. That has to be the best course of action right now. "I just stepped out for some fresh air...my head was pounding. I'm just heading back to my room to get ready for breakfast."

She looks me up and down, obviously taking in my dress and bare feet. "You stepped out for some fresh air and got dressed up in your wedding clothes?"

"They were on the chair," I say. "Anyway, I'd better get back to my room, otherwise breakfast service will be finishing." I'm past her and ten yards down the hall when she calls after me.

"I wasn't born yesterday, Bethany Blane. You watch yourself. You're not too old to get a bad reputation."

I don't bother turning because what's the point. Mom's radar is on high alert. I'm not going to explain myself to her or try to deny what is obvious.

In my room, I scramble into my coral bikini, cut-off shorts and tank top. My poor feet are grateful to slide into some white sandals. I throw a few things into my beach bag and find my sunglasses. Then I'm off to breakfast with a thudding heart and butterflies in my stomach.

Will the twins be there already? What about their brothers? I think about what mom said again. Bad reputation. There are now four witnesses to my sins. Four very sexy witnesses. Two I can believe would go a long way before outing my indiscretions. The other two, I can't be so sure. There certainly seems to be some lighthearted friction between Liam and Callum and their younger siblings. Maybe a bit of rivalry or jealousy. I wonder what it must be like to follow in the footsteps of men like Callum and Liam. They're gorgeous, confident, funny and surprisingly kind.

And I'm so damn excited to see them again.

Too excited.

I slow my pace, thinking about how fragile my heart had felt only yesterday. If you'd asked me if I'd be risking it in the hands of one man I'd have laughed. Am I really prepared to risk it in the hands of two?

If it's possible to hate your own internal voice, I do at this moment. Doubts are back. Fear is back. Thinking about everything way more than it really needs to be thought about is my usual way, and look where it has gotten me. Analysis paralysis. A life half lived because I sought the control of a cruel man who took away my choices and made me weaker as a result.

It's a terrible thing to be scared to live.

When I was a child I looked around at the adults in my family and imagined what it would be like to be free like them; no one telling you what to do; a plethora of choices; a whole life to shape. And now that I'm an adult, the very thing I used to look forward to is the thing that scares me the most.

I don't trust myself. I don't trust my ability to make good decisions. I don't trust my instincts to weed out the good people from the bad. In fact, I know I make bad choices in so many aspects of my life. I've proven myself to be unworthy of the power and freedom of adulthood time and time again.

Here I am about to do the same thing again. I can tell myself the twins are great. I can tell myself that this is just a bit of fun. A vacation romance. A clichéd fling between the maid of honor and the best man…or men, in this case, but I know myself. My heart is like an overripe fruit; swollen with hope and bruised from mishandling.

As much as I want to be the girl who can throw caution to the wind and enjoy this for what it obviously is, I don't think I'm her. I don't think I can ever be her.

I want to be her.

By the time I've thought all these complex and deep thoughts I'm nearing the restaurant. I stop and look around, thinking about what I should do. There is no way I'd be able to just avoid the twins for the rest of the trip. Not without hiding out in my room, and I don't want to spend what little vacation I'm going to get this year watching reruns of the 'Gilmore Girls'. I'm going to need to face them and tell them that I can't be with them again. Even as I think it, my pussy clenches with hunger. She's been so disappointed with sex for so long and finally, I find not one, but two men who are capable of giving her the treatment she deserves and what am I planning to do? Tell them thanks but no thanks. I must be fucking crazy.

Just as I'm pondering heading to the beach and living off fruit for the day, I feel a hand on my waist.

"You waiting for someone special?" a very familiar voice whispers into my ear.

"Because I think the wait is over," another very familiar voice whispers into my other ear. All the hairs on the back of my neck rise. My knees feel weak, as though they have gotten used to the idea that these men can hold me up, no matter what the position!

"You look good in shorts," Callum says, kissing my cheek.

"She looks good without shorts," Liam chuckles, kissing my other cheek.

I catch a middle-aged woman flanked by two small children staring in our direction. Then she winks and I blush profusely! Is it that obvious what we've been up to?

Do I have that 'just been fucked' glow? Or maybe she just thinks I'm damn lucky for being in such close proximity to two of the most gorgeous men I've ever had the pleasure of seeing in the flesh. I hope it's the latter.

"Shall we get something to eat?" I say, heading through the doors and looking for an inconspicuous table. There's a booth near the windows that looks free. If I slide in there I should be relatively shielded by the twins and their ridiculous proportions. If a hurricane passed through here right now, I'm pretty sure they would be able to provide me with enough shelter between them to survive it!

I hear their footsteps behind me as I race through the dining area, scanning for familiar faces. I catch sight of cousin Dylan in the opposite corner with this family but he's looking at his food, thank goodness. I chuck my bag into the corner of the booth and slide right in. When Callum and Liam finally catch up with me and take their seats they're looking very amused. Liam is sitting opposite, dressed in a snug gray t-shirt that leaves nothing about his drool-worthy body to the imagination.

"Are you hungry, Rio?" he asks me and for a moment I must look as confused as I am. "You practically jogged to this table." He raises his eyebrows.

"She's embarrassed to be seen with us in public," Callum says nonchalantly, as though he's reading an item off the menu, not describing my shameful truth.

"Embarrassed?" Liam feigns a lack of understanding, but I know he's realized too.

"Don't be ridiculous," I start, but when they both fix me with a 'don't bullshit us' stare, I stop and have the decency to look sheepish.

"It's not you, it's me," I say and then cringe. That's got to be the worst sentence I could have chosen.

"Of course it's you," Callum says, resting his hand on my arm. "We're absolutely fine with being seen with each other in public. You kind of get used to it when you were born two minutes apart and have pretty much done everything together for over thirty years. Also, that dude over there looks the same as me, so being embarrassed by him would be like being embarrassed by myself."

"Dude," Liam says affectionately. "I didn't realize how much you cared."

"You see…and then you gotta go and say shit like that and I feel like taking it all back," Callum says.

I watch them laugh together, the easy affection and humor they share, and I feel really stupid. All my insecurities and feelings of shame seem silly when I'm in the company of these guys. Somehow, they make everything seem like it's okay.

"You know that nobody knows what we got up to last night," Callum whispers. "All of that is just in your head and ours."

I blush and fumble with the napkin on the table in front of me, remembering all the amazing filthy things we did. I was a different woman. A wanton and sophisticated woman who asked for what she needed.

"You know that there's nothing wrong with what we did?" Liam leans in across the table and rests his hand on top of mine. I stop fidgeting and go totally still, calmed by the weight of his huge palm and his reassurances. "We're all consenting adults. We all have respect for each other. We all had a damn good time, so don't kick yourself, okay. That doesn't make me feel good. It makes me feel pretty shitty."

Callum slips his hand onto my knee. "My brother is right, for a change. You should listen to him."

I look at them both, and there's so much that I want to say. I feel like I could tell them all the strange and dark things that are in my heart and that maybe they'd be able to drive them all away. Then I feel stupid because as nice as they are, and as much as we have done together, these guys are still virtual strangers.

"I don't regret it," I say. "I'm just not sure what to feel about it and I'm not sure what should happen next."

"Well, I was thinking that we attack that breakfast buffet like the raging hungry people that we are. Then find a waiter in this godforsaken hotel and order some very strong coffee. And then maybe hit the beach for a day of doing pretty much nothing but sunbathing, broken up by the odd swim and maybe some reading."

"Sounds like a plan to me," Callum says. And before I have a chance to agree or disagree they are up and out of the booth to do exactly that. So what do I do?

I follow them. Fears be damned. I'm hungry, in more ways than one!

7

MIXED DOUBLES

I manage to eat breakfast okay with Liam and Callum. You know how awkward it can be the first time you consume food in front of a man you don't know very well and really like? Well, multiply that by two and you have my situation. I choose easy food to eat. Some yogurt, granola and chopped fresh fruit. I have good coffee and some little mini Danish as a treat. I sometimes make them at home but never for other people. The hotel ones are a little dry, but sweet anyway. The boys eat eggs and toast, talking about protein, then tuck into my pastries too! Typical.

"See, that's what I don't get. Why not just pick up the pastries for yourselves if that's what you wanted to eat?"

"Never," Callum laughs. "My body is a temple. It's just you that seems to love putting temptation in our way."

"She's terrible, isn't she?" Liam jokes.

"It's like she enjoys seeing us cave."

"I do," I say. "I'm a scarlet woman. A temptress."

Liam, who is sitting across from me, looks at me darkly. "Don't joke about that kind of thing, Miss Bethany."

"Yeah," Callum agrees, squeezing my knee under the table. His hand is so hot against the bare skin of my thigh and the feel of it so illicit in this public place. "Unless you're looking to unleash the beasts on beauty. Blood rushes to my cheeks. Shivers race down my back and just as I'm about to reply, their younger twin brothers are there, standing next to the table, looking at us all with interest.

"Is this a private party or can anyone join?" one of them asks. They don't wait for an answer, just slide right on into the booth with their plates of breakfast. For some freaky reason, they have eggs and toast too. No bacon, no sausage. Maybe it's a family thing.

"We were wondering where you were," Liam says, shifting to give the brother next to him more space.

"We had to freshen up. You gonna introduce us to your friend?" He winks in my direction and I just can't stop staring. The younger twins are really similar looking to Callum and Liam; same eyes, same straight noses and full lips, same broad shoulders and narrow hips. There are differences, though. Slightly wavier hair that they style differently and they look younger somehow. Maybe it's the cheekiness and dimples or slightly rounder cheeks. It's hard to pinpoint without getting them to all stand totally still while I play 'spot the difference' and take in all their manly beauty.

"If I have to." Liam seems to scowl, as though the idea of his younger twin brothers meeting me leaves a sour taste in his mouth. "Bethany, this is Ryan and this is Matty."

"Hey," I say, blushing. It's pathetic to be my age and still get bashful in the presence of new people. I guess if they hadn't just seen me in a very compromising position I might have been less embarrassed but there is no erasing the past, however much I might wish I could.

"Hey, Bethany," they say as a chorus.

"You're the maid of honor?" Matty asks.

"That's me." I fiddle with my napkin. "Although I think my honor might be questionable."

The younger twins chuckle but Callum and Liam don't look pleased. "Don't say shit like that." Callum sounds genuinely unhappy with me.

"You don't need to put yourself down, sweetheart," Liam says.

"Yeah," Ryan adds. "Don't be thinking that we're thinking anything about your honor because of what we saw."

"It's not the first time," Matty adds, chewing a piece of toast seriously.

"Won't be the last either, hopefully." Ryan grins and takes a sip of his coffee, holding my gaze in a way that pretty much confirms what the boys hinted at in their hotel room. I look down at my legs and wonder what the hell these gorgeous men see in me. I mean, I know I have nice hair, pretty eyes, and a good smile. My legs are okay too, but I'm no super model by any means. I think my girlfriends back home may just think I'm a rabid liar if I showed them pictures of these men and told them what was on the menu; starter, main course, dessert, and coffee! Oh my goodness.

"You hinting, little brother?"

"I can ask outright, if you like," Ryan says, looking directly at me. I have no idea what to say or do at this point.

"I think you might be scaring Bethany, dude," Matty says.

"Ah, don't be scared, baby. We know what we're doing."

I stare at him with my mouth open like a fish. We're in a hotel breakfast room and, if I'm understanding him correctly, I think he's talking fivesome sex so blatantly that I'm sure the elderly couple behind us have heard. They're about ninety years old and look like they are very hard of hearing so you get how loud this discussion is.

"Chill out, bro," Liam almost growls. "This isn't the time or the place."

Ryan shrugs, reaching out to steal the last Danish. "I don't mean anything bad, Bethany. You can take it as flattery if you like."

"Yeah." Matty glances across at me and smiles almost shyly. "My brother's not trying to railroad you into anything. He just liked what he saw and wants to see more."

"He wants to do more than look by the sounds of it," Callum says. He's looking at Ryan with an expression that seems almost proud.

"I'd settle for watching if that's what's on offer?"

Now I'm blushing even harder, remembering that moment when I needed something to help me come and the realization that someone was watching was enough to push me over the edge. I've always had a secret little fantasy that involves a man sitting in the shadows, watching me have sex. If one man can make me come hard in my fantasies at my own hand, what would two men in the shadows and two men giving me direct pleasure do? And why the fuck am I thinking about this now? When I look up from my plate there are eight eyes fixed on me.

"What?" I ask them.

Callum leans in close and strokes my cheek. "Just ignore them, okay." I blink, feeling a lump rise in my throat at the softness in his eyes as they search my face. I will not cry because he's treating me kindly. It's been so long since I felt tenderness in a man's touch that tears well in my eyes. "Shit." Callum puts his arm around me and I bury my face in his chest. "Look what the fuck you did," he growls.

I pat his chest and shake my head. "It's not that," I say against the warm cloth of his t-shirt. He tips my chin so I'm forced to look at him again. I get lost in his eyes that are steely and concerned. "What is it, sweetheart? Tell me."

I shake my head, so conscious of where we are and the other brothers surrounding us.

He's so warm and solid and I press my face back against his heart and breathe deeply.

"It's the way you're being with her," Liam says quietly.

Callum doesn't respond but strokes my hair gently and I stay in his arms until I've swallowed down the tears. I'm kinda mortified to face everyone after my burrowing, but when I sit straight and look around, they all look so worried about me that my mortification slips away.

"There she is." Liam smiles softly. "Back in the real world."

"The real world sucks most of the time." Matty shrugs and smiles lopsidedly. I know he's trying to make the situation light and I really appreciate it.

"It really does," I say.

We're all quiet for a while and I fiddle with my napkin again. I didn't mean to take all the fun out of the day. I'm not a drama queen or a particularly serious person. I'm not a fragile person either. Not by nature.

But I know I'm a little broken and the cracks are starting to show.

"It doesn't have to, Bethany," Ryan says. He's watching me closely now with a look on his face that tells me he's trying to figure me out. He's edgier than the other three. Obviously very determined too. It's as though he's seen me, decided he wants me and isn't going to let the idea go. I get the feeling that he's trying to determine the best way to achieve his objective. There's no way I'm going there, but I can't help feeling a little flattered.

"Let's change the subject, okay?" Liam says quickly. "Where the hell is dad?"

Matty and Ryan glance at each other and I don't miss the flash of warning in their eyes.

"He's resting in his room. He said he'd meet you later," Matty says.

His statement might be true, but for some reason, I'm thinking there's more to this than meets the eye. Dan told me that Callum and Liam have been out of the states for work. What kind of parent doesn't immediately come to see their kids who have been away from home for months? My mom might be one of the most difficult people I have ever known, but she takes her parental responsibilities seriously, even if it is just to keep face.

"Look, boys. We're gonna take Bethany down to the beach and chill for a bit. I think she might need a bit of space," Callum says, looking at me for confirmation.

I nod my head. I want to put my sunglasses on and soak up the sunshine. I want to forget that I have bits that need gluing back together in order for me to function as a normal human being.

"We'll see you later for dinner," Liam says, patting Ryan on the shoulder.

"Sure," Matty and Ryan say at exactly the same time. We all slide out of the booth and I hang to the side while the boys all shake hands and talk about cool places to go on the island. I catch Ryan looking over at me and he smiles slightly, cocking his head to one side. It's a look that says, 'I'm not a bad guy' and I believe him. From my experience of Callum and Liam, they are men who know what they want and go after it. I shouldn't expect anything less from their brothers, I suppose.

When all the chatter is over, both Matty and Ryan come towards me to give me a peck on the cheek.

And I notice the funniest thing. The all wear the same cologne.

8
BEACH BABES

I know I'm getting funny looks from people. I can feel the curious stares and the sneaky side-glances. It isn't me just being paranoid. Well, I don't think it is anyway.

I'm lying on a sunbed flanked by two identical twin gods. When we arrived at the beach, Liam and Callum found us a spot at the front that I was grateful for, because now I don't need to try and walk across scalding sand while trying to maintain my dignity. I was planning on going at the end. Let the boys be together so they can talk and I can mainly pretend to be asleep while my brain goes at a hundred miles an hour over everything that has happened in the last twenty-four hours, but that didn't happen. Guess they like me sandwiched between them!

It's been nice. Too nice. Funny conversation. Butterflies in my stomach every time either Liam or Callum look or smile in my direction. I put breakfast behind me, but every so often, I get a flutter in my chest at the thought of Ryan and his determination, and Matty and his shyness.

What is it about gorgeous men that seems to knock the sense out of women? I mean, I'm pretty sensible in real life, but put me in a booth with Adonis, his twin and his practically identical younger brothers and suddenly I'm like emotional soup. Or pudding. Or something else equally squishy and unsuitable for functioning in day-to-day situations.

Well, a day on a Caribbean beach is hardly a day-to-day situation. It's paradise here. Everything I imagined it would be when Kerry showed me the website. The sea is a gentle shushing sound. Children's laughter drifts on the breeze. Whenever I turn over I have a man ready to rub in my sun cream. I don't even have to ask.

I think it's the cream rubbing that's causing the stares. First Callum smoothed it all over my back and legs. When he eased his hand in between my thighs to coat the sensitive skin there, I almost moaned. It wasn't that part that would have raised eyebrows, though. It was when Liam insisted on rubbing cream into my front. I mean, I can do that myself with no problems. Who asks someone to smooth cream over their belly, for fuck's sake. When he started towards my cleavage, I quickly slid off the sunbed and hurried into the sea. I could hear him laughing behind me, probably thinking that I'm a prude in public.

It's hardly surprising, is it? This may be an enlightened era when it comes to sex, but ménage relationships aren't exactly a regular thing. Maybe Callum and Liam are so used to sharing that they've forgotten what normal is.

I don't get to hide in the sea by myself for too long.

"Hey Bethany," I hear from behind me.

I turn towards the shore and spot Callum and Liam wading out. Oh holy hell. This is dangerous.

"Hey," I say watching them like a deer would a pair of wolves. Liam picks up seawater in his big palms and splashes it over his face and hair. Callum does the same. Droplets of water run down their torsos, following the grooves between their muscles. As Liam gets closer I can't stop staring at a water droplet that has formed on the end of his right nipple. It just hangs there, waiting to be licked off. I want to lick it off, but if I thought people were staring before, then they'd be getting the popcorn out for the main event if I did that.

The twins get even closer and dip down into the water so we're all now at eye level. When they're in front of me I know I'm safe. I'm a good swimmer. I can swim out deeper and escape if they try any funny business. It's when they split up and come at me from both sides that I don't know what to do.

"Guys," I say in a voice laced with warning.

"What?" they both say at the same time.

"Just remember where we are, okay?"

"Last I checked it was Jamaica," Callum says.

"You know, the beautiful Caribbean Island," Liam says.

"Very funny. You know that isn't what I meant."

They both shrug; an attempt to maintain their innocence, but then I feel Callum's hand on my waist and Liam's hand on my hips and I flush scarlet.

"Don't," I say, trying to wriggle away.

"No one is watching, honey," Callum says.

"They are!" I plead.

"Who?" Liam looks around and I follow his gaze, expecting to catch a few of the people closest to be staring in our direction, but no one is. They're all too busy enjoying their own vacations.

I blink as Callum's hand slides over my ass, giving it a good firm squeeze. The slip of his touch over my wet skin feels amazing.

He comes closer until his face is next to my ear. "You know, you are even sexier when you're shy," he says. "Makes me want to get even dirtier with you to make you blush."

"She's blushing already," Liam says, coming even closer. "I bet if I did this…" He slides his hand around and cups my pussy under the water. "She'd blush even more."

"She'd do more than blush," Callum says. "She's gonna gush."

And he's right. I can't even pretend that they aren't making me wet. If I wasn't in the sea it would be ridiculous. This whole situation is ridiculous. I can't let them do this to me here, as much as I want to, and I want to so much it's an ache.

"We can't do this."

They both stop for a second. Liam cocks his head to the side. "Are you really that worried about what people think?" There's a little flash of hurt in his expression that surprises me. These two men seem so self-assured, so 'larger than life'. There's no way I was expecting either of them to feel hurt by my unwillingness to indulge in public displays of affection.

"It's just…" I stutter over what to say to make things better, and then I hear my name.

"Bethany, honey." It's my mom and I practically leap away from the twins and head towards her voice. It's not that I want to see my mom. After what she said to me this morning quite frankly I'd prefer to avoid her all week, but that isn't going to be likely.

"Hey, Mom," I call. She looks pretty ridiculous in a straw hat and sunglasses, but mom is obsessed with maintaining a pale complexion to stave off the wrinkles.

"The sea is just beautiful," she says, glancing over my shoulder. "Ah, you're with Liam and Callum," she says in a voice that sounds a little weird. Uncertain.

"Yeah. We're just hanging out."

"Hi, Mrs. Blane," they say, coming closer.

"It's Ms.," she says primly.

There's a moment of silence as we all stand awkwardly, then Callum saves the day with some wedding talk.

"That was a beautiful day yesterday. We thought we were going to miss it after all the flight problems."

"Yes," mom says. "We were worried you would, too."

"Thank goodness we didn't," Callum says. God, they sound so formal.

"I didn't know you were friends with Bethany," Mom says, narrowing her eyes. She has that look she gets when her radar is picking up something she hasn't quite worked out yet.

Suspicious.

"Yeah. Just from yesterday. Thought it'd be good to hang out," Liam says.

"Well," Mom looks between us all. "Bethany's not going to be around much. We have family obligations." I want to say 'huh' because I have no idea what she's talking about. There haven't been any arrangements made as far as I know. "You know Cousin Dylan. He'd really love to spend more time with you, Bethany."

Now I know something is up because Cousin Dylan has never been a fan of mine. I think it's because our moms played competitive when we were growing up. 'Bethany got this in her exams'. That kind of thing. He was generally on the losing end of those kinds of discussions, which is probably why I get a frosty reception any time I try to talk to him.

"I've got a few days left, Mom," I say.

She looks between the twins again suspiciously. "Why don't you come and sit with me for while?" she says to me. We can go and get a mimosa."

"Okay," I say. "I'll get my sarong." I turn to the boys. "Are you going to stay at the beach all day?"

They nod, eyes seeming to size me up in the same way as my mom's had. They must see that I'm happy to accept mom's invitation so that I can escape from them for a bit. I just need that headspace.

"Well, I guess I'll see you later then."

"We'll be here," Liam says.

The walk back to my sunbed is awkward. I can feel the twins' eyes on me. I know they're watching and the thought of it makes me hot between my legs. Public displays of affection might be a problem for me but imagining hot threesome sex, not so much. I decide to take my bag too so that I can reply to a few messages using the Wi-Fi.

Mom is waiting at the beach bar, wearing a flowing dress.

"Here, darling," she says gently pushing a tall glass towards me. The bubbles in the champagne tickle my nose as I take a long drink.

"Thanks, Mom." Perched on a stool, looking out over the beach, my eyes are drawn back to the twins. They're playing in the shallows with a ball, and even from here I can see the ripple of their muscles as they hit it back and forth. Damn.

"They're good looking boys," Mom says.

I snap my head in her direction and see her looking thoughtful. "I guess," I say.

"No guessing needed," she says. "Every woman on this beach is thinking the same thing."

I must blush because she laughs. "Hard to choose when there are two." I choke a little on my latest mouthful of drink. "Anyway, I'm going to make that situation easier for you."

"What situation?" I ask, frowning. Mom isn't usually this cryptic.

"I got engaged this morning," she says. For a moment I just stare at her blankly. Engaged. What the hell does she mean?

"What?"

"I've been dating a lovely man for a while now. He arrived here this morning. He proposed and I said yes."

She beams, looking younger than she has in a long time and I gawp, the things she just said not really penetrating my brain. I didn't even know she had a boyfriend, let alone that they were thinking long term.

"Who is he?"

She brushes some sand from her arm. "His name is Frank," she says. "He's amazing. You're going to love him."

"Okay."

"And we're going to be a huge family."

"What do you mean?" I say.

"Well, he has four sons."

Wow. Four stepbrothers. That's going to be interesting.

"Two sets of twins, actually," she says looking down the beach towards where Callum and Liam are now sitting at the edge of the sea, soaking up the rays.

"Two sets of twins," I repeat, my mind sliding over the coincidence. So weird, I think as I take another sip.

"Yes. Ryan and Matty, and Callum and Liam."

I spit the mimosa that's in my mouth all over the sand in front of me, coughing and sputtering. What in the actual fuck?

"So you see," she continues. "No point in choosing between those gorgeous boys when they're going to be your new family.

And just like that my world comes crashing down again.

9

DOUBLE BUBBLE BURST

I should have known that good things don't happen to me. Any time I find a scrap of happiness, something swoops in to steal it away. Any time I try to step out of the safety of my boring everyday life, I'm smacked in the face. I don't know what mom thought of my extreme reaction to her news. After coughing and spluttering my mimosa everywhere, I made an excuse that I needed to clean up and disappeared back to my room. I sat in the bottom of the shower for half an hour, completely distraught at the news that not only have I slept with my soon-to-be stepbrothers, but I had threesome sex with them. Oh god.

I can never come back from this. There is no way we can all get together for family dinners and holiday get-to-togethers, and I can just pretend that nothing happened. They made me come harder than I've ever come in my life.

My face flushes scarlet at the thought. I pull on panties and a bra, then slip on a soft white cotton dress and flop onto my bed to wallow in my own misery.

This is a disaster of epic proportions.

Not only have I slept with two of my stepbrothers, but also the other two witnessed it. They've all seen me naked.

I groan and cover my face with my hands. This is just too awful for me to think about. For a second I wish that Kerry was here, but would I tell her? She's my sister and I've always confided in her about my life. But this? This feels like too much for me to take on board, let alone Kerry.

I'm still lying in the fetal position half an hour later when there's a knock at my door.

It must be mom, I think. Coming to check that I've gotten over my coughing fit. But when I open my door, my twin problems have come to life.

"So this is where you are," Liam says, looking me up and down.

"We were waiting for you to come back," Callum says.

I stand, clinging to the door and not quite opening it enough for them to come in.

"You gonna let us in or should we just talk in the hall?"

"I don't think it's a good idea," I say. My face must look as grave as I feel because Liam puts his hand on the door above mine and eases it open.

"You don't look good, baby girl. You sick?" he asks, stepping into the room and resting his hand gently on my forehead. I gaze up at him, those gunmetal eyes so pretty and now laced with concern.

"I'm not sick," I say.

"Then why did you disappear without saying anything?" Callum asks, closing the door. They're both so tall and I feel tiny and stupid. Stupid for allowing myself to act on my base instincts. Stupid to trust my ability to make sensible decisions for myself, when what I actually need to do is do the exact opposite of what my brain and heart are telling me.

I don't even know how to answer Callum's question. Do they know? Did they know before we slept together that our parents were dating? Fuck! Maybe that's why they went after me so hard. A kinky thing. Let's fuck our stepsister. I actually feel sick.

"Mom told me something. I just had to come back here."

"Bad news?" Liam asks. He rests his hand on my shoulder in concern.

They seem so genuinely worried that I can't imagine that they knew. Maybe they still don't. Should I be the one to tell them? I just don't know what to say.

"Good news for her. Bad news for me." It's the truth.

"Tell us, honey. Whatever it is, we can help you deal with it."

"I really don't think you can," I say.

"Try us," Callum says smiling gently. "We're pretty good listeners."

I take a few steps away from them and go to sit on the edge of the bed. "Mom told me she's getting married." They move in closer, curious. "I didn't even know she was dating."

"Okay," Callum says. "And you don't want her to get married."

"No, it isn't that," I say. "She deserves to have her own life…her own happiness."

"So what is it?" Liam asks.

I glance between then, trying to find the words to communicate this big and horrible thing. In the end, I go with the 'ripping off the band-aid' option. Quick and painful.

"She's engaged to your father."

I think we're all frozen for at least a minute until Liam seems to emerge from the coma of shock. "Our father?"

"Yep. That's what she told me. I think she could see I was crushing on you, so she pulled me aside to let me know you're all going to be my…" I struggle over the next word. "Stepbrothers."

"Fuck," Callum mumbles. From their reaction, I can see for sure that they had no idea. That's a relief. At least we are now all shocked and horrified together and for the same reasons.

They both draw themselves up and look at each other. I watch as they seem to communicate silently in that way that only twins seem to be able to manage, gauging each other's reactions and thoughts from expression and body language alone. Then they turn back to me.

"You seem upset," Callum says.

I frown. Is he not?

"We're going to be related," I say, not sure why that statement needs articulating at this point.

"By marriage," Liam says.

"Yes."

"But not by blood, honey,"

"You're going to be my stepbrothers," I say. What is it about this that they're not getting?

"But we're not right now," Callum says, coming closer. When he sits on the bed next to me and his thigh presses against mine, I'm torn. My body remembers how it feels to have his skin against mine, his hands caressing, and his mouth kissing. My mind remembers the rushes of pleasure. My heart remembers how lovely they made me feel; how beautiful and treasured, how special and deserving of the wonderful way they treated me. "And even when we are, what difference does it make?"

I raise my eyebrows because I can't believe he can be so nonchalant. "Thanksgiving dinner, family events. It's going to be so awkward."

Liam crouches in front of me. "Is it awkward now?" He rests his hands on my knees, his thumbs pressing into my soft inner thighs. He still has a little sand on his forehead and I want to brush it away from his tan skin, but if I touch him, I know that I won't be able to stop.

I nod my head, keeping my hands clasped together in my lap.

"You're serious?" he asks, sliding his hands up my legs a little and cocking his head to one side. I know what those hands can do to me and it's all I can do not to shiver. Those eyes of his are dark gray and penetrating now, seeking my true feelings through my protestations. I don't know what he sees because I don't truly know what I think or how I feel. It's all just too much for me to take on board.

I nod and he cups my cheek. Callum's hand takes hold of one of mine, forcing me to unclasp my fingers. I gaze at them, my eyes wide. I expected them to walk away because what have we really shared?

One amazing night.

Half a day that didn't feel real.

Snapshots of moments where I felt more understood by them than I've ever felt before, but it's all an illusion painted over the reality of a one-night stand, isn't it?

"Don't regret what we did," Callum says.

"Nobody has to know anything," Liam tells me. "We don't ever discuss the private parts of our life with anyone."

"Except for each other." Callum grins slightly.

"What he means," Liam says, "Is that you don't have to worry about anything getting to anyone else's ears."

"And what about your brothers?" I say, raising my eyebrows. "They got to witness plenty today."

"And they won't say a thing either!"

"How can you be sure?"

"Because they know we'll kick their junior asses if they do," Liam chuckles.

"I think they have a bit of a crush on you," Callum grins.

"Jealous little punks," Liam adds.

I look between them, not really following what they are saying completely. I'm suddenly very intrigued about their younger brothers. Do they share women like Callum and Liam? Have they ever all shared one woman?

The thought of so much gorgeous man has heat surging between my thighs and on my cheeks.

"She's blushing," Liam says, running his finger where my face feels hot.

"You thinking dirty thoughts, baby?"

I shake my head, trying to think of something to say that will distract them from all this.

"She is."

"Can you blame her?" Liam rises, taking my hand and pulling me to stand too. He rests his big palms on my hips and bends to kiss my neck. It feels so good that I want to moan but that would only encourage him. I put my hand on his shoulder to ease him back. I can't take this level of temptation and think straight.

"You don't have to worry, baby," Callum repeats. "We'll take care of you."

He's close behind me now, his breath gusting on my neck in a way that sends a shiver up my spine and across my bare shoulders. His lips press against the sensitive skin there and I feel like jello. My eyes drift close just before Liam's lips meet mine. They're so soft and teasing, sucking gently until I feel dizzy. Two sets of lips worship me, while two pairs of hands caress my curves. It's as though they mapped me out last night and now they know all the places to stroke and squeeze that drive me wild. Callum's hands slip from my waist up over my ribs until they cup my breasts, squeezing firmly while he whispers how good I feel. When he pinches my nipples through the fabric of my dress and bra, I push my ass against him.

He's hard against the seam of my ass, his dick as rigid as a night-stick, and my pussy clenches at the knowledge, remembering what it felt like when he pushed that big thing inside me.

"Do that again," Liam whispers, but I'm not really sure what he's referring too; Callum squeezing or me moaning and bucking. Callum tweaks my nipples again, harder this time while Liam watches. His eyes are burning. "Lift your skirt, baby," he says. "Let me see your panties."

I do as he asks, using both hands to grasp the hem of my dress and lift. I have cute panties on. Little lace things that leave nothing to the imagination. For a second I wonder what the fuck I'm doing. All my regrets and doubts are still there, but the sex fog that these men seem to be able to cast over my brain has made them seem much less important. Liam groans as he looks between my legs.

"Sit on the bed, Callum," he orders his brother, his eyes bright as though he's thought of an amazing idea that he just has to put into action. Callum lets go of me and does as his brother instructed, pushing his shorts down to reveal his beautiful cock.

Man, I could write poetry about that cock. The way it stands proud and straight. The gorgeous color of it. The soft roundness of the tip that helped to ease its way inside me. He sees me staring and smiles. "It's all yours, baby. Come and get it."

"Not so fast," Liam says. "I've got plans for you." He kisses my mouth hard, teeth nibbling my bottom lip as he turns me and backs me towards his brother. I hear the tear of foil and the snap of latex and know that Callum is getting ready for me. I'm already ready for him, the slipperiness between my legs trickling into my panties. Liam's hand goes between my legs, pushing the thin strip of lace to the side. "You gonna sit on my brother's cock?" he asks me, pushing a finger up inside me so far I end up rising up on my toes.

"Yes," I whisper, feeling Callum's hands on my thighs, pushing up my dress so he can get a good view of my ass.

"I've got you, baby," Callum murmurs. Between the two of them, I'm lowered until I feel the tip of Callum's cock pressing against my entrance. He's so big that it feels almost impossible, but I open around him, the weight of my body pulling me downward. Liam opens my thighs until my legs drape over his brothers', my hands braced on my knees for stability. His eyes are between my legs, fixed on the point that Callum and I are joined.

"Fuck," he whispers, kneeling in front of us. "Ride him, baby. Let me watch."

I start to move with Callum's hands supporting me, raising up and rolling my hips. He feels so good, so perfectly huge and stiff that every movement presses a spot deep inside me that makes me gasp with pleasure. "Oh..." I look down between my legs as Liam licks a finger and presses it onto my clit.

"Go slow," he says. "Let me see it all."

So I do. My thighs burn as I move upward, allowing the full length of Callum's cock to slide almost out of me, then down, down, down until I'm fully seated in his lap.

"Oh fuck," Callum says as I squeeze myself tightly around him. Liam's finger circles gently, but it's his gaze between my legs that has me so turned on I can hardly breathe. Knowing that he's watching. Knowing that he can see my pussy spread around his brother's cock is so unbelievably sexy. It should feel wrong to like it. He's going to be my stepbrother soon, but I can't find it in myself to care right now. It should feel wrong that my clit feels like it's gonna burn from his touch, but it doesn't.

"You're so beautiful," he says, holding my gaze while he circles gently.

"She feels so good," Callum says from behind me, nipping my shoulder with his teeth.

"I need to go faster," I say, feeling my orgasm approaching like a slow-moving wave.

"Slow," Liam insists, putting his free hand on my hip and gripping. "It'll be more intense if you go slow."

"Listen to him," Callum urges, gripping my waist and controlling my movements. Oh...it feels so good I drop my head back and just feel.

"That's it," Liam says. "Just lose yourself."

I do as he says, breathing deep and letting every little sensation build into something so big it's almost frightening. Callum's hands move to my breasts, squeezing and pinching at my nipples until I can't hold myself back. I buck onto his cock as deep as I can take it, bending forward to kiss Liam while he keeps his fingers against my clit. "Oh, oh, oh..." I moan against his lips.

But it's when I feel Callum's cock start to swell that I know I'm gonna come.

It starts slow, a low rumble of pleasure that spreads from my center and outwards until I'm arching my back, gripping onto one of Callum's hands and one of Liam's, riding out the waves.

Callum groans as his own orgasm hits, and Liam talks through the whole thing; sweet and dirty things that make everything sharper and more vivid. When we've both stilled, it's Liam who stands and helps me up on shaky legs. He cups my cheek in his palm and smooths my sweaty hair. "You were perfect," he says. "Now it's my turn."

I shiver as he turns me, pressing his hand against the small of my back until I'm bent at the waist with my hands resting on the bed. It's seconds for him to sheath himself, then he's using his fingers to spread open my labia, taking his time to look at my wet, pink opening. The air cools against my pussy but not for long. Before I know it, he's pushing his way inside me. It's so odd to be filled so quickly by another cock that feels so much like the first. No man can be ready to go a second time in such a short time frame. My pussy is swollen and wet and the penetration so deep that it knocks the air from my lungs in a whoosh. Liam's not gentle and I understand why. He's been watching and waiting and now he's taking his pleasure. I can admit that there is something unbelievably sexy about being used this way. The press of his fingers into my hips is brutal and the noises he makes are tinged with an edge of desperation that makes me so hot.

Callum is there next to me, his hand holding onto mine, his lips seeking mine as though he wants to swallow my moans. Liam's cock is so impossibly hard now, and even though I'm getting sore I can already feel another orgasm rising inside me. It's different than the first, faster and scarier in a way, as though Liam has reached deep inside me to yank it out. "Oh fuck," I shout as it surges from between my legs like a flash. I feel wetness trickle down the inside of my thighs and for a moment I'm mortified. Did I pee myself? I know that can happen during sex. Liam groans as he comes, leaning his weight over me, pressing his face between my shoulder blades. As he slows, he makes a happy sound.

"You're so wet, baby. You came like a river."

"You made her squirt." Callum chuckles and I look at him, confused. "Sometimes a vaginal orgasm can make a woman ejaculate," he explains like a medical professional. I must turn red because he laughs again. "Nothing to blush about, Bethany. It's sexy as hell."

As if to illustrate the point, he smooths his finger between my thighs, slicking in the evidence.

Liam slips out from between my legs and I go to stand, wanting to get to the bathroom to clean myself up, but neither of the twins will let me disengage.

"Come here," Callum says, pulling me towards him until I'm straddling his lap. "You smell so fucking sexy." He holds my face between his palms and kisses me sweetly, sipping at my lips as though I taste of honey. Liam strokes my back and kisses the top of my head softly. The way they touch me after sex is so reverent. Worshipful almost. I feel blissed out and soft-boned, so when they encourage me to lie on the comforter between them, I do. I'm not planning to fall asleep. It's still early in the day, but I must do because when I next open my eyes the room is dark and someone is knocking at the door.

10

RUDE AWAKENING

The knocking is loud, as though whoever is out there has been banging a while. I blink, looking around, finding Callum and Liam stirring next to me. I'm naked, except for Callum's arm that's draped over my middle and currently cupping between my legs. Jesus.

"Bethany." My mother's voice barks from outside and I practically jump out of my skin. I know she can't get in here to witness this scene but that doesn't stop me from feeling the wash of shame and fear.

I can't open the door with the boys in here. I'm just going to have to wait for her to leave.

"Bethany," she calls again. Why does she always have to be so persistent? It's like her mom-style Spidey sense is able to detect me through wood and concrete.

The knocking stops suddenly and I let out the breath I'd been holding. I look between the boys who are lying totally still and silent, ears angled towards the door. Then my phone starts to ring.

Shit.

My mom knows what I'm like. I don't ever go anywhere without my phone. She's gonna know I'm in here hiding from her.

"Bethany, I know you're in there. Open the door."

I stand and shuffle off the end of the bed, reaching for my silk robe that's resting over the back of a chic-looking curved chair. I don't know why I'm bothering to cover my nakedness because I'm not letting her in, but it seems wrong to talk to her through the door naked.

"Mom, I'm not feeling well," I say close to the door.

"Open the door," Mom barks again.

"I'm sick, Mom," I say. "I don't want you to catch it, okay."

"Vomiting?" she squawks. She's always had a phobia, which is why I'm using it as my excuse.

"Yeah. Maybe food poisoning."

"Oh, that's a shame," she says. It sounds like sympathy and I'm surprised momentarily until she adds, "I was going to tell you to come to dinner with Frank and the boys. A celebration."

I actually do feel nauseous now.

"I can't, Mom. I'm going back to bed."

"Okay, sweetie. We'll postpone it until tomorrow. Frank hasn't been able to get hold of the older twins either. They seem to be missing too."

I hear rustling behind me as the twins swing their legs off the side of the bed and start to find their shorts.

"I'll see you tomorrow, Mom."

"Get well, Bethany," she calls and I hear the sound of her heels moving down the hallway.

I shuffle back toward the bed, but this time my instinct isn't to push the boys away. I need to hold them close because this thing we have feels like it's going to drift away. "Your dad is looking for you," I tell them as Liam comes to slip his arms around me.

"You're shaking," he says, smoothing my sex-mussed hair away from my face.

"I'm okay. Just…"

"Just scared out of your ever-loving mind."

Callum places his hand on my hip and kisses the top of my head.

"She's not going to find out, okay?"

"You don't know my mom. She's got x-ray vision. She can see through doors and hear sounds from ten miles away."

"She's not going to find out," Liam says firmly.

"And what about dinner tomorrow? How is that going to work out?" I ask, exasperated.

"We all sit around and talk like normal human beings because we are normal human beings," Callum says. "Just because we've had amazing sex, doesn't mean we have that stamped on our forehead."

I shake my head because they don't get it. Maybe they're used to this kind of thing. I have no idea how many times they've shared a girl in the past or what kind of relationships those were. They can be flippant because this isn't new to them, but it is new to me.

I just can't get past the bubbling shame I feel. It doesn't matter how much I like them or how good they make me feel, I know that being sexual with both of them at the same time is wrong. The trouble is that knowing it hasn't stopped me from acting on my urges. If anyone found out about this, especially mom and her new fiancé, I would never be able to look them in the eye again.

My family life would be over.

Mom would never forgive me for ruining her 'new life'.

"I'm not that good an actress," I say.

"Could have fooled me," Callum says. "Your mom bought that little food poisoning ruse hook, line, and sinker."

"That was through a door. She'd have realized I was lying straight away if I'd been standing in front of her."

"Look. There's no point in stressing about all this," Liam says firmly. "We're a little too far into the situation to have regrets. We just need to make sure that there is no reason for either your mom or our dad to be suspicious. And believe me, we'll work hard to make everything appear totally normal."

I take a deep breath and hold it, trying to push the anxiety away from my heart.

"Okay?" Callum asks.

I nod.

"We should go," Liam says. "We need to go find dad and the twins. Find out what's going on."

"What are you going to do about dinner?"

"We could get you something and bring it to your room."

As if my stomach senses the prospect of food, it growls loudly.

"I'll get room service," I say. If I can reduce the risk that someone might see the twins around my room, I will.

"Okay, Rio," Callum says, bending to kiss me gently on the lips.

"We'll see you soon," Liam says and kisses me too.

For a second, I'm so damn grateful that they somehow came into my life.

But then, when they're gone, I feel empty inside, like my heart already knows that it's temporary and it's going to be aching again soon.

11

SPOTLESS MIND

I have a salad for dinner and watch a stupid rom-com on the hotel's entertainment system. I even break open the mini-bar and drink up all the gin in the fridge with ice-cold tonic. I'm feeling very sleepy when there's yet another knock on my door.

Jeez. Who the hell is it now?

I roll off the side of the bed feeling more than a little woozy and go to stand close to the door.

"Who is it?"

"Ryan and Matty," a deep voice says from the other side of the door. "Liam sent us to check on you."

I frown, wondering what the deal is, but I decide to open the door because keeping it closed in my soon-to-be stepbrothers' faces feels ruder than I'm prepared to be at this early stage of family bonding. Still, I'm wary of their motivations since the conversation over breakfast.

"Hey," I say, taking in the sight of one of the twin's baby brothers. Not such a baby.

Damn.

These O'Connell boys are all way too sexy. They must create quite a stir when they go out together. It's just so hard to separate them all in my mind when they look pretty much identical.

Ryan cocks his head to one side, just as Liam does. "You look a little flushed. Are you sure you're not really sick?"

I think about what he and Matty stumbled in on this morning and flush even more.

As if reading my mind, he smirks. "I told you that you don't have to be embarrassed around us. It's not the first time we've seen something like that and it won't be the last."

Oh god, let the ground swallow me up. I'm totally mortified and it must show.

"You're a beautiful girl, Bethany," Matty says gently. "Any guy would be grateful for having seen you naked."

"Oh my god," I squeak. "Do you have to?"

Ryan chuckles, deep and low. "You know what? You look even sexier when you're embarrassed."

"I don't think this was quite what Liam had in mind when he sent you guys to check on me."

"Probably not," Ryan says. "In fact, he gave us a lecture about conversational content before we set out, but Liam doesn't get to control everything or everyone, as much as he might like to."

Sounds like there's some serious sibling competitiveness going on between these two.

"So how come he sent you?" I ask.

Matty shrugs. "He didn't have much of a choice. Dad insisted that Liam and Callum spend some time with your mom. Kind of a 'get to know you' exercise. With our brothers having been in Dubai, they hadn't met dad's girlfriend. Me and Matt have spent some time with your mom already."

"So how long have you known about all this?" I ask, wanting to find out how long my mom has been hiding things from me.

"Oh, they've been dating for a year I think, but the engagement was a surprise."

"A year!" I practically screech. "She's been hiding this from me for a whole year." They both shrug like they have no idea what to say. "What kind of mother doesn't tell her adult daughter she's dating someone for a whole year?"

"Seems like she's a secretive woman, doesn't it," Ryan says. "Are you a secretive person, Bethany?"

"What do you mean?" I ask, feeling a little defensive.

"Well, Callum and Liam told us we need to keep what we saw to ourselves. Seems like it's not just your mom who likes to play her cards close to her chest."

"That's hardly the same thing," I say.

"Isn't it?"

Matty steps forward a little, as though he can tell his brother is starting to wind me up. He'd be right.

"Of course it isn't. She didn't tell me about her one serious boyfriend. You're talking about me keeping two guys I've had a vacation threesome with a secret. Definitely a different thing."

"I think my brothers see you a little differently than you see them," Ryan says with his eyebrows raised.

"What do you mean?"

"Well, Bethany. Just so you know, my brothers don't share girls they aren't taking seriously. That isn't how it works. They're okay with having casual sex separately, because they aren't thinking the girl might be something longer term. But if they both like a girl enough for something more meaningful, then they want to share because they know they don't want to live apart long-term."

Ryan's expression is fierce, as though talking about his older brothers has made him protective. For all his directness and challenge, seeing this side of him makes me feel less hostile. Particularly when Matty puts a hand on Ryan's shoulder and squeezes.

"We're the same," Matty says softly. "We tried to date separately, but it just caused problems between us. Dating isn't something we're prepared to let come between us anymore."

I don't know what to say to any of this. I never intended for what I had with Liam and Callum to be anything more than a fling, but as stupid as it is to be happy that maybe they are thinking longer term, I am. If circumstances were different, I think I could love them. It's a pretty terrifying thought. The way I feel about them after such a short amount of time has me reeling. The fact that their brothers are telling me that they could feel the same is terrifying and beautiful, all wrapped up into one uncertain package.

There are so many things I want to ask Ryan and Matty, but it feels like prying. Before I get a chance, Ryan rests his hand on top of the door frame and smiles. His eyes are heavy-lidded, his grin sexy, and I get the definite impression that he's about to turn on the charm.

"You wanna go for a walk on the beach with us?" he asks. "Seems a shame for you to be stuck in this room when it's so beautiful outside. The others have gone to a restaurant in the hotel next door so we won't be seen."

I should probably say no and go back to my solitary sad evening, but with mom otherwise engaged, a walk on the beach sounds much better than being cooped up in this room. I'm going to have to get to know Ryan and Matty at some point now that we're becoming a strangely blended family, so it seems like as good an opportunity as any I'm gonna get.

"Sure. That sounds nice. I'll just grab my purse."

My sandals are on the floor by the dresser and my purse is on a chair by the window. I'm ready quickly and Ryan and Matty have politely stayed in the hallway to wait.

"So, you came to surprise your brothers?" I ask as I close the hotel room door.

"Well, we knew that dad was going to propose to your mom and that Liam and Callum would be here for the wedding, so we thought it was a good opportunity to bring us all together. My brothers aren't due back in the US for another couple of months so this seemed like a good time to have a reunion."

"It's nice that you all want to spend time together."

"We're really close," Matty says. "When we're all in the same area, we tend to do everything together." He smirks and I get a feeling he might be talking about something more than going to grab pizza. Or maybe that's what he wants me to think. I've no way of being sure without asking him outright. "When we moved out of home, we all got an apartment together. Poor pop was a bit lonely for a while, then he met your mom and now he's glad to have the house to himself."

I shake my head because I really don't want to be thinking about the reasons why their dad might want to be alone with my mom.

"So you all live together? Aren't Callum and Liam living away?"

"They're in Dubai right now on business. Our company is in the running for a big security contract there."

"Oh, wow," I say. "Security." I don't really know what it entails but I don't want to pry too much. "That must be interesting," I say.

"Well, it's never quiet, that's for sure. We're bidding for some big contracts in some of the South American countries right now. It's close enough for us to be at home on a regular basis, though."

"So you all still have a place together?"

"Yeah," Matty says smiling. "We all get along really well."

I wonder for a moment what it might be like to be a fly on the wall at casa O'Connell. Are they tidy or is the place like a college frat house? Do they all sit around watching TV in their underwear? Then my mind wanders back to my main point of fascination with these men. I know they don't always share girls, and I know they do share in their twin pairs, but do they ever go so far as to share between four? I want to know the answer so badly but there's no way I'm going to ask. Instead, I get back to making innocuous conversation. "That's nice. I'm close with my sister too."

"Kerry? We haven't met her yet."

"I'm sure you will soon."

We're almost to the beach, walking through the lush gardens planted to the rear of the hotel. I can smell the damp saltiness of the sea and the sweet scent rising off the evening-warmed flowers. It's beautiful and romantic and I get a pang that Callum and Liam aren't here too. That they're having to spend the evening schmoozing my mom makes me even more resentful of the ridiculous situation we're all finding ourselves in. I mean, parents getting remarried when kids are young is one thing, but parents expecting that their new relationship is going to bring together six adult kids into a family unit seems deluded.

"Did your mom give you the 'we're all gonna be family' talk?" Matty asks, cutting a glance at me curiously. It's like he was reading my mind.

"Yeah," I say. "Four new stepbrothers," she told me.

He chuckles. "I bet that came as a bit of a shock."

"You could say that. Especially when I found out who the stepbrothers were."

"Especially after what you've been getting up to with my brothers, you mean." Ryan's eyes flash with mischief and even though I was thinking the very same thing, I still blush scarlet.

"Yeah, about that..." I say. "You know that if my mom found out, she'd probably never speak to me again."

"Yeah," Matty says softly. "We get that."

"So you'll keep what you saw to yourself?"

Ryan shrugs, ushering me through the walkway to the beach. "What did I see?" he asks with a wink.

I smile, but I'm not really convinced by his pretense. I feel as though Matty can be trusted, but there is something about Ryan that is still jarring to me. Something sharp and challenging. I play along, though, because that's what I think he's expecting. "Nothing, I guess. My mistake."

When my shoes touch the sand I stop and lift them, slipping off my sandals so I can feel cool grains between my toes. We walk towards the sea and then along the shore. The moon casts a stream of yellow light across the inky water and it's so beautiful that my heart aches a little.

"There's something so melancholy about you," Matty says softly. "Something sad. I didn't see it before, but I feel it now."

"You feel it?" I say, trying to sound skeptical. Ryan is looking at his brother and something passes between them in the hushed silence of the deserted beach. I wish I knew what it was. I wish I could decipher twin eye contact because the more time I spend with the O'Connell brothers, the more useful I think that skill would be.

"Yes," Matty says. He stops walking and sits on the sand, slipping his own feet from his brown leather sandals and leaning back on his arms. I stand, looking out towards the inky horizon, wondering at what he said. Do I really give off that aura so obviously?

"You can sit, you know," he says.

He's smiling and patting the sand beside him. Ryan sits now too, taking a place next to his brother. In the low light, with their hair fixed just like their older brothers, Ryan and Matty look uncannily like younger mixtures of Liam and Callum.

I take a seat next to Matty, crossing my legs and folding my hands in my lap the way I always do when I'm not really sure of the situation.

"Sadness is a burden to carry, Bethany," he says softly. "I know because I carried it for a long time after my mom died. I couldn't seem to let it go. I guess we all deal with things in different ways. My brothers partied harder and looked for distractions. Maybe because I'm the youngest I felt and dealt with the loss slightly differently."

"How?"

"I withdrew. I put barriers up. I was fearful of letting people close because I didn't want to feel that loss again."

I sigh and he rests a hand on my forearm and gives it a gentle squeeze.

"I know you don't want to hear it because I felt the same, but you need to know that putting barriers up will hurt you more in the long run. You have to accept the risks that come with caring for someone, because otherwise you won't ever reap the benefits that come with opening yourself up to loving and being loved in return."

I'm still after he's finished because I feel so exposed. Ryan's sitting with us, listening to the whole thing, and I get the feeling he'd be the kind of man who'd think that this kind of conversation was stupid. I thought I was better at hiding things but here I am finding out that my vulnerabilities, my fears, my weaknesses, are all on show to this man who is, for all intents and purposes, a stranger. I can't find the strength to respond, particularly when I can envisage Ryan scoffing at anything I might reply that would involve feelings. So we sit together in silence for a while, me digesting what Matty has said. I have no idea what he's thinking outside of what a sad and fucked up individual I am. This whole situation feels seriously strange. I'm not a curiosity for the O'Connell brothers to fix. I've got two of them thinking that amazing sex will cure me of my hang-ups, and another two trying to psychoanalyze me on a dark beach. Well, maybe only Matty is trying to do that. Ryan only seems concerned with getting me into bed.

I start to feel a bit pissed off that they can be so presumptuous. We've spent so little time together.

"You don't know me," I say quietly, but the warning tone is clear in my voice. It doesn't seem to dissuade Matty, though.

"I know," he says. "But that doesn't mean I don't see you, Bethany."

"And you can see all that from the way I walk? The way I talk? What?"

"You carry yourself so you don't ripple the air. Your shoulders are tight, your steps measured. You're so closed off."

"Not so closed off," I say. "Your brothers can tell you that."

He shrugs his shoulders and gazes out to sea. "Sex is one thing. Being free to give your heart is another."

"Maybe I've got good reason to keep my heart to myself," I say.

"Maybe you have," Ryan interjects. "But, maybe you should know that my brothers care about you."

"They don't know me," I say defensively.

"Don't they?"

"From a few conversations and some sex? I don't think so."

"I think you underestimate the impact that a few conversations can have if someone is really listening."

I think back to the night before. The way that Callum and Liam seemed to see and react to the things I said and the things I didn't say. The way they'd look at each other before changing the way they responded to me. What Ryan is saying is true. I did feel as though they were getting inside my head. But it's dangerous to be thinking that what we've been doing has been anything more than a two-night fling, as much as my traitorous heart might be feeling otherwise.

"It doesn't matter either way," I say shrugging my shoulders.

Ryan's stare is penetrating and dark. "You can tell yourself that, but I know that you don't really mean it."

"And how do you know that, Mr. Expert in everything me?"

He shrugs and grins, seemingly totally unphased by my snarkiness. "My brother has a gift for getting to the heart of people. I don't need to look that deep to see everything I need to know."

I turn and face them, shifting my legs to the side so I can get a proper look at these men who presume to see me.

"Why did you come and find me?" I ask.

"Because that's what we do," Matty says. He shrugs, and when Ryan looks like he's going to speak, he puts his hand up to stop him. "I don't know why we're like this," he says, but Ryan makes a scoffing sound. "Well, maybe I do."

"Our mom was a family therapist," Ryan says. "We grew up listening to her talking about understanding people...taking the time to see to the root of people's motivations and drivers. She spent a lot of time helping other people, and for whatever reason, it seems that my brothers have inherited her predilection." There's a bite of anger in his voice and Matty puts his hand on Ryan's forearm.

"Some of us respected what she did."

"I respected her," Ryan snaps. "Just didn't really like the way she put everyone else first."

"That's not fair," Matty says.

"No point in going over this again," Ryan says, standing and walking closer to the shoreline. His shoulders are high, his body coiled tight, and for the first time, I feel like I see through his hard outer shell.

"She sounds like an amazing person," I say softly to Matty. He stares at his brother as though he wants to go to him, but I guess that years of experience have taught him that it won't help, because he stays right where he is.

"You're looking for something, Bethany," Matty says.

"What am I looking for?"

He shifts forward, moving closer, then reaches out to touch my face. "Love. Understanding. Fulfillment. Same as we all are."

"Then why are you so bothered…if I'm the same as everyone?"

"Now that is the interesting question."

I frown as he stands and reaches for my hand. I reluctantly stand too, bending to collect my purse and shoes. "Not interesting enough to answer, though," I say.

"I'm not sure you're ready to hear yet, Bethany."

"I'll tell you what I am ready for," I say, turning and starting to walk back in the direction we came.

"What?" he calls, seemingly not trying to follow.

HUGE X4

"My bed," I say. "I'll see you around."

12

DOUBLE DISAPPOINTMENT

The next day, mom is at my door bright and early. I squint at her through sleep-blurred eyes and she huffs. "Look at you. This really won't do."

She strides forward, her hand pushing on the door to make enough room for her to pass through. Typical mom. No asking if she can come in. Just barge right in.

She's a cloud of white caftan and strong perfume, obviously making sure she's extra glamorous for her new fiancé. I, on the other hand, still have sand between my toes from last night's stroll and sex-mussed hair from the shenanigans with the boys yesterday. For mom, appearances are important, and mine will be telling her all sorts of unpleasant things about my general state of mind. No one in the family is ever allowed to tarnish the veneer of perfection she has created.

"Are you feeling better, darling?" she asks. There isn't really any concern in her voice to match the words. This is all about her finding out if I can fall into line and do the meet-and-greets with Frank and the boys later.

"A little," I say, not wanting to lay my cards on the table. If there is a chance I can avoid it, I will.

"Well, that's good. You need to eat and drink something now. Get your strength back up."

As if my stomach is ruled by my mom, it rumbles loudly.

"See!" she says, looking intensely vindicated.

"Okay, mom. I'll order room service."

"Don't be ridiculous," she says. "The buffet is lovely and included in our stay."

"But I'm not dressed, mom." She looks disapprovingly at my shorts and camisole pajamas that are adorned with pink and white hearts.

"It'll take you five minutes to have a shower and throw on a sun dress. I don't mind waiting."

And to show me that I have no choice she takes a seat on the chair by the vanity and pulls a book from her purse.

I trudge towards the bathroom, feeling defeated. I'm a grown woman who lets her mom rule her life. Why can't I just say 'no mom, I don't want to go down for breakfast right now?' It should be easy. I would with anyone else, but I have a lifetime pattern of giving in to her and I can't seem to break it. Even though I know I'm going to spend the next few hours fuming with disappointment at myself, it's easier to face that than defy her.

I scrub quickly and wash my hair, combing the tangles away. The hotel towels are like clouds on a summer's day and I wrap a huge one around myself and pad back into the bedroom. Mom looks up from the pages of her romance novel and gazes down her nose at me.

"Better," she says. "Sometimes all a person needs is a shower to make them feel better."

I nod and seek out a clean summer dress from the small closet. I find some dry swimwear and head back to the bathroom to get ready. In the mirror, I notice all the things about me that have aged; less roundness to my cheeks and fine lines at the corners of my eyes. I'm young but I feel worn out from dealing with difficult people. I feel disappointed that I still can't seem to fight my own corner. I put a little bronzer on my cheeks, nose and the middle of my forehead. Just enough to look sun kissed. Then I swipe on some waterproof mascara. My hair will dry wavy if I leave it, but there seems little point in straightening it to go out into the humidity.

"I'm done, Mom," I say, slipping my feet into some sandals. She's up and ready in seconds, breezing towards the door.

"Come on then, Bethany," she calls over her shoulder. "Time's a wasting."

And I trail after her like the good little girl I am.

In the hotel breakfast area, I glance around for the twins and find them sitting in the same booth we had the day before. Liam sees me first and smiles. There are three other dark heads in the booth too. The rest of the O'Connell brothers are there too.

"Let's get something to eat and we can go join the boys," Mom says. There's a softness to her voice that shocks me. Then I understand. She always wanted a son. She used to tell me that when I was little. When I was older she confessed that she wasn't able to have any more children after me, and I always felt that she blamed me for that, as ridiculous as it sounds. Is it a coincidence that she's found a new partner with four extremely manly sons? I doubt it. And I'm dreading the purring she's going to be doing over all of them. She loves the attention and it's all just going to make me cringe.

I spend ages looking at the buffet, pretending to choose something that my stomach can handle. Mom is huffing and puffing because I'm taking so long. When I feel like I can't stall any longer I grab a croissant and a bowl of fruit salad and trail along behind her as she glides towards the twins.

"Good morning, boys," she says loudly. "Can we join you?" They all smile and shift in the booth, clearing space for us to put our plates on the table in front of us.

"Morning ladies," they all say in a chorus.

Somehow I've ended up next to Callum and he wastes no time in sliding his hand up my thigh and giving it a squeeze. My pussy clenches involuntarily and I have to hold in a moan because I know what those fingers are capable of doing to me. His eyes are glinting with mischief when I turn to give him a warning glare.

"So, how are you all doing this morning?" Mom asks.

"Fine thank you, Ma'am," Ryan says, nodding politely.

"That's good," Mom says breezily. "Bethany, have you met Ryan and Matty yet?"

I nod and she smiled. "It's such a gorgeous day. Nice to see youngsters getting up early to make the most of it." I don't miss her pertinent glance in my direction at that. Seriously, she thinks I was ill and still there is zero sympathy or understanding. Callum squeezes my leg as though he can tell I'm getting tense. If he's noticing my mom's dig then it's not me being paranoid.

"It is a gorgeous day, and I'm glad to see that Bethany is feeling better today," Liam says, smiling broadly.

I nibble on my croissant gingerly. "A little," I say.

"That's good. Enough to get to the beach?"

"Maybe," I say.

"Do you think that's wise?" Mom asks, her eyes narrowing. She glances at Callum, specifically at his arm that is closest to me. It's like her eyes can see through wood to his gentle caress on my leg beneath the table. Maybe it's me that's giving something away. Does my face look relaxed? I'm usually so tense around her. Maybe that's my mistake.

"I'm sure Bethany knows if it's too much for her," Callum says cautiously. It's so sweet that he wants to stick up for me, but is trying not to rock the boat with mom.

"Bethany has a tendency to overreact to things," Mom says, popping some fruit into her mouth and smiling.

"Like what, Mom?" I say, feeling totally humiliated.

"Would anyone like more coffee?" Matty asks in a blatant attempt to change the subject.

"I would," Liam says.

"Me too," Callum agrees, draining the last of his to emphasize the point.

I'm quiet, looking at my plate so I don't have to look at mom, feeling totally shamed by her comments that seem designed to make me look small and stupid in front of the twins.

"Like my engagement," Mom says, finally replying.

I look up at her immediately, finding her sitting with a smug expression on her face that I want to slap away. I know I shouldn't feel like that about my own mother, but it's at times like this that preserving any kind of respectful daughter pretense becomes almost impossible.

"Your engagement?" I splutter.

"Don't think I'm stupid, Bethany. You come down with a mysterious illness when I want you to come and meet Frank and the boys."

"What?" My voice sounds high pitched as I struggle to keep it together. Is she really going to do this now? Air all our dirty laundry in public. It isn't really like her to do anything to sully the family name. Then I get it. She doesn't want the boys to like me. She's jealous that they might actually want to be my friends. She wants their attention all to herself.

"It was very convenient," she says, brushing her hand over her hair.

"I don't think…" Liam starts, looking at me worriedly.

I raise my hand to stop him because I'll be damned if I'm going to sit here and let her walk all over me, even if she is right about what I did. "Do you know what, Mom? I wasn't expecting any sympathy from you because you don't have a sympathetic bone in your body. A lifetime's worth of experience of having you as a mom has taught me what to expect. But to sit here and call me a liar in front of complete strangers, well, that's just totally unacceptable. You think the world revolves around you and your plans, but it doesn't. And you know what? I'm done. I'm done letting you hurt me. I'm done being disappointed by the way you treat me. I'm done hoping that our relationship might be different one day, and I'm done sitting here with you."

She doesn't even flinch at my tirade, but when I go to get up she hisses at me to sit.

"No, Mom. I won't sit. I won't pretend that we're something that we're not. Welcome to the family, boys," I say, waving my hands between mom and I. "Happy days all around."

Then I drop my napkin on the table, grab my bag and leave the restaurant.

My hands are shaking and my heart's thumping in my chest. I actually feel physically sick from the confrontation. As I make my way back to my room, my mind whirs to try to comprehend how this is going to change my life back home. Since I moved out of my apartment with Brad, I've been living back with mom. There's no way I'm going to be able to go back to that arrangement after all this.

I'm almost at my room when I hear footsteps behind me. "Bethany." It's one of my twins, I think and then blink. My. Where did that come from?

I turn and Liam and Callum are there, striding down the hallway. Their faces are serious with concern and in that moment I realize that I need them. I need their arms around me and their whispering voices to tell me everything's going to be okay. But I shouldn't. I shouldn't be needing them at all. In a day or so they'll be going back to Dubai and all of this will be nothing but a memory. Being on my own scares me so much and I hate my own weakness.

I wrap my arms around myself, trying to find the strength to hold myself separate from them. I don't want my heart to be bruised again. I'm barely recovered from the last round of heartbreak. The trouble is that they don't seem to feel the same way. When they're close enough, Liam immediately pulls me into an embrace that has my cheek mashed against his pec and my whole body sagging in relief. My arms unfold instinctively to wrap around his narrow waist. Callum's there too, stroking my back.

"Your mom was totally out of order," Callum says.

"She should never have said those things, especially in front of all of us," Liam adds.

Callum bends to kiss my head. "I don't know what she was thinking," he says, and the burning lump in my throat just grows each time they speak.

"She wanted to make me look small in front of you," I say quietly.

"Well, that isn't what she achieved," Liam says.

"Exactly," Callum says. "If anything, it was the opposite."

"You did the right thing to stand up to her." I grip onto Liam's shirt, feeling so relieved that they support me. The last thing I'd want them to think is that I'm a disrespectful person, especially to my mom. That isn't how I've been raised at all.

"I bet she was spouting steam when I left," I say, cringing.

"She mumbled something under her breath when we made our excuses to leave."

"What if she followed you?" I say, pulling my hands from around Liam's waist and resting them on his chest to ease myself back.

"She still had a lot of breakfast to eat," he says, kissing my head.

"Don't worry, she's not going to find out about us," Callum says.

I relax again but it's only momentary.

"Us?" a deep voice says from beside us. The twins jump to attention almost at once, and I turn to see who has spoken and am confronted with an older salt 'n' pepper version of Liam and Callum. Frank?

Oh shit.

"Hey Dad," Callum says. Frank's eyes narrow, taking in the scene he has obviously just witnessed a whole lot of.

"Bethany, I assume," he says.

I nod, taking a step away from the twins as though a foot of distance might somehow make him forget all he saw and heard.

"What the hell do you think you're doing, boys?" he says, and the anger in his voice is vicious. I can see them recoil a little and I feel terrible. This was exactly what I feared would happen. I know they are grown men who can make their own decisions, but I also know what it feels like to deal with the disappointment and anger of a parent, and it isn't good.

Neither of them says anything and that just seems to enrage Frank even more. "Both of you?" His startling gray eyes flick between them. Seems like he knows about their sharing tendencies too. This is just mortifying.

Again, neither of them answers. Callum slips his hands into his pockets, and I wonder if it's because he's worried about lashing out at his dad the way I felt the urge to do with my mom. I glance at Liam and his fists are balled. It's instinct that makes me step forward.

"Mr. O'Connell," I say, reaching out a hand. "It's nice to finally meet you. I'm sorry that I couldn't make it last night. I was sick," I say.

Frank looks at my outstretched hand like he may not shake it, but then he seems to reconsider. His hands are just like his sons but with thinner skin and more pronounced veins. His grip is strong and he doesn't let go. Instead, he leans in, holding my hand tightly. "I'm only going to say this once," he hisses. "You stop whatever it is you're doing with my boys and leave them alone, for your mother's sake."

He drops my hand like it's something dirty and I stare open-mouthed at this man who looks so much like the twins but is obviously very different in character and manner. "Dad," Callum says in a warning voice, stepping forward and putting his hand on my arm.

Frank raises his finger and jabs it violently. "Now you listen here, boy. You are not going to mess this up for me, do you hear."

I shrug Callum's hand from my arm and start running down the hallway, feeling utterly humiliated. I hear raised voices behind me as the twins start to respond to their father's outburst and I'm glad that they're not going to follow me. I just need to get away.

In my room, I lean against the closed door and rest my hands on my knees, taking deep breaths to try and calm myself. The humiliation. I have never felt like this before. I'm too mortified to cry even, and it's then that I realize that I just need to get on a plane and go. I need to disappear before any of this escalates into more shouting and accusations. All my worst fears have been realized and it's time to make a break for it, while I still can.

I grab my suitcase from the closet and start to pack my things frantically. I'm almost done when there's a knock at the door. Apart from Kerry, who is on the other side of the island, there isn't anyone that I want to talk to right now. I ignore the next set of knocking too as I gather my toiletries in the bathroom.

"Bethany," I hear, thinking the voice sounds like Callum. There's a sharper, more demanding edge to the way he says my name, like that one word can convey the importance of me opening the door for him immediately.

I want to. So badly.

But I can't.

If I let them in, I know what will happen. They'll try and convince me that we've done nothing wrong and that it's our parents who are behaving badly here, not us. They'll make me feel better by making me feel safe, and I can't let them do that. I'm already too hooked on them for my own good. The thought of getting on a plane and not saying goodbye has my stomach clenching and my heart aching. They'll hate me for bailing. I know they will. But it's for the best. Maybe, in a year's time we'll all have moved on and 'family' occasions won't be so fraught. Although my mom has treated me appallingly, I don't want to ruin her new life. From what I can see, she and Frank are made for each other, and I never thought I'd be able to say that about a man. They deserve each other, well and truly.

And what I deserve is some peace. To forgive myself for falling for Brad's manipulation. To forget how it felt to be worshiped by Liam and Callum. To get away from my mom and her toxic influence in my life. Most importantly, to find myself and be happy being single.

"Bethany." I think it's Liam this time. "Come on, babe. Open the door. We just want to see you and make sure you're okay.

They bang again and I know I'm not going to get rid of them without reassuring them at least.

I go nearer and press my hand against the door. "I'm okay," I tell them. "I just want to be by myself, okay?"

"Open up, honey. We're so sorry about our dad. Just let us in so we can talk."

"I can't. Please." I wait, wondering if they heard the crack in my voice through the slab of wood between us. A single tear drops down my cheek as I imagine them walking away. The sadness inside me is so big and consuming that I find my hand pressing against my heart.

"Bethany," they say together, and I can almost feel the connection of their hands on the other side of the door.

"Please," I say again, and then I slide down the wall until I'm curled in a ball, my ear pressed against the wood. I hear them talking; just a murmur of voices. They're trying to decide what to do next. I know they don't want to go. I know they were hoping they could convince me to let them in, to my room and maybe to my body again. The way they've been with me I wonder how they're feeling in their hearts too. I recall what Ryan said about the boys not sharing unless they're thinking about more than sex with a girl. If that's the case, then pushing them away like this feels doubly harsh.

They debate some more and then stop. I think they're leaving but then a note is slipped under the door, right at my feet. I reach forward to retrieve it and find it's a receipt from the hotel bar for three cocktails. Our first night. The note is short and reads, "We're so sorry you're hurting, Bethany. Don't push us away. Come find us later when you're feeling up to it."

Another tear rolls down my cheek and I swipe it away quickly, scrambling to my feet. My hand reaches for the door handle, but just as I'm about to turn it, I stop.

13

RUNNING INTO TROUBLE

I'm running away. I know this. It feels wrong in so many ways, but right too. I make it to the airport without issue, my new return flight booked and quick journey in a taxi to take me away from my troubles. I'm dressed in the same clothes I threw on for breakfast, tugging my hastily packed suitcase behind me while I look around for the correct desk. My phone rings in my handbag but I ignore it. If it's someone I want to speak to then I'll call them back later when I'm departure-side and I've had a chance to have a gin and tonic and relax. If it's someone I don't want to speak to then I will just ignore their attempts to get in contact. Nothing is going to draw me into a conversation that I know is only going to serve to make me more upset. I see the flight desk I need and start in the direction of the overly made-up woman who is staffing it, when I hear my name.

It's a male voice and my heart sinks. Was I spotted leaving the hotel by the twins? I can't face them here and now. It's just too damn hard. I keep walking and hear feet thudding behind me. Then a hand is on my shoulder and I'm forced to stop.

"Hey, Bethany. Wait up."

It's not Liam or Callum, so I turn.

It's either Ryan or Matty but I'm not sure which. I haven't had a chance to figure out a way of separating the younger twins yet.

"Matty," he says as if he can read my mind.

"Hey," I say, not knowing where to look. His eyes are taking in my suitcase and the direction I'm heading, and putting two and two together. I guess what I'm doing is pretty obvious.

"You going somewhere?" he asks, slipping his hands into the pockets of his loose linen trousers. His eyes are just like his brothers but his mannerisms are different. He seems more uncertain, but I suppose that could be because he doesn't really know me.

"Yeah. I have to head home."

"Oh," he says. "I thought you were going to be staying for a few more days."

"It's work," I lie. "They need me to come back to deal with a crisis."

Matty doesn't say anything for what feels like an age. His eyes scan my face as though he's trying to decide if I'm telling the truth or not. Even I know that my story sounds pretty suspect, particularly as he witnessed the confrontation with mom earlier.

"Do Liam and Callum know?" he asks eventually.

I don't want to lie to him about that. It's a step too far. "No…it's all been a bit of a rush."

He frowns. "They'll be pretty sorry about that."

My heart sinks but I smile brightly. "I'm sure they'll be fine. Plenty of other gorgeous girls in the resort for them to have some fun with.

Matty's frown deepens. "You really think that's what they'll be thinking about when they find out you've gone?"

I shrug because I don't know what to say without making myself sound more callous or them more shallow.

He takes a deep breath. "Bethany, it's pretty obvious this isn't about work."

I blink and open my mouth to protest, but again I just can't find it within myself to defend a lie. I sigh and stand my suitcase, using my now free hand to rub my forehead, trying to figure out what to say.

"I just couldn't stay, okay."

"Because of your mom?"

"Because of everything."

"So you're going home. Isn't that going to be a temporary fix?"

"What do you mean?"

"Well, you live with your mom, don't you? She's going to be home in a few days."

I sigh again because Matty's right. I'm only escaping her wrath temporarily. In fact, I think as soon as she finds out I've left she'll be jumping on the next plane out of here, just to make me feel even more guilty about ruining her vacation.

"Two days is better than no days," I say, sounding defeated.

Matty looks thoughtful, then he digs around in his bag and pulls out a set of keys. "Look, this might sound crazy but you're welcome to stay at ours, just until the dust settles."

I must look completely stunned because he grins. "It isn't an offer I'd make to just anyone, but seeing as we are going to be family soon, it seems like the right thing to do."

"I don't need your charity, Matty," I say.

"Why do you have to be so defensive all the time?" he says. "Not everyone is out to hurt you, you know."

His comment floors me because he's right. He's made a sweet and genuine offer to help me out and I'm just being horrible and rude. He shrugs again, as though opening his home to me, a practical stranger, is something completely normal. I look at the keys that are dangling from his hand and think about how great it would be to have somewhere to hide from mom and the situation, just for enough time to get my life sorted out. It'll take time to find an apartment for myself. This could give me that time. Plus, I know that Liam and Callum are going back to Dubai so I won't be putting myself in a difficult situation. When Matty and Ryan come home, I'll be working and I can try and stay out of their hair as much as possible. All I need to be able to do is keep a polite distance.

"Are you sure?" I ask, and he nods.

"I wouldn't have suggested it otherwise. Look, take these." He holds the keys to me and I extend my hand so he can pass them to me. He rummages in his bag again and comes up with a pencil and a luggage tag. He scribbles something on it. "The address. It's not too far from where your mom lives."

I take the tag and read his gorgeous cursive. The apartment is in a great and really convenient for my business space. This could work out so well.

"Really?" I ask again, feeling like I need to give him a little time to make sure he isn't doing something totally crazy.

"Absolutely. Stay in the first bedroom on the right. That's Liam's."

"Okay." I get a shiver imagining slipping into Liam's bed, sleeping in the room that houses all his personal effects. I'm not the kind of person to look through someone's belongings, but I'm totally intrigued to find out what pictures he has up. Maybe his closet will smell of his cologne.

"We'll be back in two days. Our numbers are all on the board in the kitchen if you need anything. Just make yourself at home."

I nod. It's only then that I realize that Matty's at the airport and I haven't asked him why. Did he follow me? "How come you're here?" I ask.

"My suitcase was sent on the wrong flight. I came down here to collect it now that they've managed to find it."

"Ah," I say, feeling relieved.

We stand awkwardly for a moment, then he steps forward and kisses me on the cheek. His lips are soft and the kiss is strangely tender under the circumstances.

"You take care, Bethany," he says and then steps back.

"Thanks, Matty," I say with a lump in my throat. For a moment I wonder how someone as awful as Frank managed to raise four sons with so much empathy. All I can think is that their mom must have been one amazing woman to leave such a legacy.

"I'll see you soon, okay." He turns and heads off in the direction of the information desk and I watch him go. In his tight white t-shirt, his broad shoulders and biceps are impressive. Everything about him from behind looks exactly like his older brothers; same dark hair, same tapered waist, same walk that is purposeful with just a little bit of swagger. I can't help but pine a little for my twins who are going to be so far away soon. I have no idea when I'm going to see them again.

I head to check in my luggage and then proceed through security and passport control. It's only when I'm on the other side that I head to the restroom, sit in a cubicle, and allow myself to cry.

14

ROOM WITH A VIEW

I take a cab from the airport, reading the driver the address from the luggage tag and watching the streets go past. We eventually pull up in front of an impressive looking apartment building and I get out, taking a look around at the neighborhood.

There are some pretty amazing cars in the lot, and a nice grassy area for residents to enjoy in the front of the building. The entrance is glassy and modern. The taxi driver retrieves my suitcase from the trunk and then I head up the path to my temporary refuge. I haven't turned on my phone since I landed and to be honest I'm feeling a little scared to. I'm pretty sure mom will have left a very angry message. I may just delete it without listening to it, but I'm most worried that Liam and Callum will have called too. Matty definitely would have told them about our chance meeting and the fact that he's offered me a place to stay. I wonder what they'll think about the whole situation.

Maybe they'll be angry I left. I wouldn't blame them for that.

Maybe they'll be glad that Matty stepped in to help me.

Maybe they'll be weirded out by the idea of me being in their space. If I switch on the phone I'll find out, but at the moment I just feel like burying my head in the sand.

The lobby smells of lilies and there's an elevator at the back that I head toward. I know theirs is apartment 3c so I press the button for the third floor. It's so weird to be dragging my suitcase towards a strange door and even weirder to unlock that door with an unfamiliar key, but it's opening the door that really freaks me out!

I peer into the apartment and I'm greeted with a typical man-cave. Brown leather sofas, massive wide screen TV, fancy juicer on the granite counters and about fifty pairs of huge shoes on shelves beneath the coat rack. It smells fresh, like an alpine forest in the sunshine and, as I push the door closed behind me, I feel immediately at home. There's a gorgeous built in bookcase that's stacked with CDs, worn paperbacks, and trophies. I leave my suitcase standing in the hallway and start to nose around, laughing aloud at some of the pictures on the shelves. Four little boys sitting cross-legged on the grass, four little boys holding ice-creams on the beach. Four grown men with their arms slung around each other's shoulders as Liam and Callum graduate. A beautiful woman sitting on a sofa with a toddler on either side of her and two babies in her arms.

I get a lump in my throat at that. I can't imagine what hard work it must have been to have four boys under the age of three. Their mom looks tired but happy. I see her in the boys so much. Mainly in their facial expressions.

Something about their smiles comes directly from their mom.

I move on from the photos and chuckle at some of the books on the shelves. Dan Brown and Stephen King I would expect, but 50 Shades of Grey and Men are from Mars, Woman are from Venus I would definitely not! I chuckle, wondering whose reading material they are, then realize they're most likely something left behind by an ex-girlfriend. My gut clenches with jealousy at the thought of them having other women in this apartment.

Any of them.

That's a complete and utter revelation to me because I'm not generally a possessive person yet here I am feeling resentful about a fictional woman, and covetous over four men. I shake my head, thinking that I really need to pull myself together.

I shuffle towards the corridor, still chastising myself for thinking such ridiculous thoughts, and open the first door on the right.

Wow.

Liam has some serious taste. His room is something else. Rich. Masculine. Super sexy. A dark wooden sleigh bed in a giant size dominates the room. The wall behind the bed is midnight blue and the rest of the walls are white with black and white pictures in dark wood frames. He has a huge desk in front of the window where I can imagine him on a laptop, lounging back with his hands behind his head, gazing at the view.

It is so perfectly him. I walk around slowly, looking at everything as though I'm an explorer who's stumbled on an ancient tomb. All the artwork is beautiful photography of natural settings. I love that he's put so much thought into decorating his space. It's grown up and stylish and makes me attracted to him even more. I didn't think that would be possible!

Then I do what I swore I wouldn't do, and peek in his closet. I immediately get hit by the scent of him and it does funny things to me. Like Pavlov's dog, but instead of salivating I get hot between my legs. It's not as neat as the closets you see on those MTV crib-type shows, but it is pretty orderly and there seems to be a little bit of space for me to hang up my clothes.

I go back into the hallway and drag my suitcase into Liam's room. I have only my vacation things with me so I'm gonna need to head home in a bit to collect a few more of my personal possessions. Not too much, though because I'm not planning on staying for too long. The last thing I want the boys to think when they return is that I've moved in for good.

I place my case on the bed and unzip, beginning to sort out the dirty laundry from the clean clothes. I pull out the underwear I was wearing for the wedding and gaze at it wistfully. Who knew it would see so much action? Who knew it would witness the start of such a big change in my life?

I hang a few dresses up in the closet and line my shoes up next to Liam's much larger ones. I linger, leaning in to smell his clothes again and feel such a pang of longing. This wasn't supposed to happen. I wasn't supposed to feel anything for the twins. It was meant to be a fling but somehow they wriggled under my skin and now I'm feeling things that are dangerous.

My phone is on the bed beside my purse and I walk over to get it, holding it and staring at the blank screen. Am I brave enough to turn it on and deal with the fall out of my decision to leave early? I stroll back into the kitchen to get a glass of water while I decide. It's cool and fresh and makes me feel a little better. Bracing myself, I power up the phone and wait. It takes a minute for the beeping to start. Voicemails. Messages. Emails. It seems that as soon as I turn off my phone I become popular.

My Facebook notifications show that Kerry has been uploading photos of the wedding, so I look at those first. I know I'm avoiding the inevitable but I don't care. The pictures are amazing. Kerry and Dean look so in love, my heart swells for her. There are some of the ceremony and then I flick to one that shows me flanked by Liam and Callum and I want to cry. I look so uncertain in the image and the twins are both gazing at me with smiles on their faces, full of confidence and oozing charm. The way I felt at that moment was so unsure. Unsure about how I felt about life and myself, and remembering that makes me realize that I do feel different now, even just a little. More confident and a little braver. Those are definitely good things.

I finally decide I need to listen to my messages. If I can be the kind of person who wants something and goes for it regardless of the consequences, then I can face up to those consequences.

The first message is mom, as predicted. Her voice is high-pitched from the first word and I delete it immediately. There is absolutely no point in putting myself through that. The next message is Kerry. She's heard that I've left and is sad that she didn't get a chance to say goodbye. She wants to know what's been going on and tells me to call her. The next message is Callum. His voice is strained when he says he can't believe that I left without saying goodbye. He pauses and I wait, my heart pounding in my chest. Then Liam is there. He tells me to make myself at home in his room, to stay as long as I need to, and that the next time they see me they want me to be in a happier place.

HUGE X4

When the message ends, I realize I'm in a happier place already. Just being in their space makes me feel content, even though they're not there. It's as through the essence of them is enough to relax me.

15

HOME ISN'T WHERE THE HEART IS

I head home in a cab to pick up some warmer clothes, my laptop, and other personal items I think I won't be able to do without during my stay at the twins' apartment. I look around at my room and feel sad. It's never been a place that I've been able to relax in. As kids, Kerry and I would escape to our rooms whenever mom was in a particularly awful mood, which was often. I don't think she ever really got over the humiliation of being left by dad. I'm not the tidiest person and my room was always a major thorn in her side and totally out of synch with the rest of the immaculate house. I've always felt like she was annoyed with me and like I had to pretend to be someone different.

When Kerry moved out to live with her first husband, I felt like my only ally had left me behind. For whatever reason, mom seemed even more disappointed with me at that point, probably because I didn't have a boyfriend.

When Brad came along, I think I just jumped at the idea of having someone. Mom loved him because he was rich and commanding; I think she would have liked him for herself, to be honest. She practically shoved me out of the door when I asked if she thought it would be a good idea to move in with him. In retrospect, I don't even know why I asked her. Maybe I was pleased that finally, I was doing something that she approved of. My grades had always been a disappointment to her, my career choice not impressive enough for her to brag about to her friends. Even when I was featured in the local paper for my cakes and won a state competition, she'd only been begrudgingly congratulatory.

I was little when dad left. I still have no idea why he went. I have no idea if he ever tried to see us because mom would never talk about him. Any questions about it were ignored and then she'd be horrible for days to make sure we knew what would happen if we broached the subject again. The day she found out he passed away, she announced it with no emotion and no sensitivity towards us. That night, Kerry came into my room and slept in my bed. We didn't talk about it much but she told me she wished she'd gotten to ask him how he could have walked away so easily and never looked back. I wanted to know the same thing. Mostly, though, I would have told him that I didn't blame him and that I understood.

It doesn't take me long to put the things I need in a small suitcase. It'll take a whole lot longer to move the rest because this time I won't be coming back again. I need to grow up and stop relying on mom to bail me out.

My most important items go in a large shoulder bag. My order book, my recipe book – not that I need to refer to it much these days – and my baking equipment. I take the things that I can't do without. Most of it is in my small studio, but I had some things at mom's so I could work on sugar crafting in the evening.

I flick through the order book quickly and find that I have a few for next week. I can get ahead now that I'm not going to be vacationing as planned. My heart sinks. I'd been looking forward to a holiday for such a long time and it feels pretty damn disappointing to be standing at home when I should be in a bikini on a beach in paradise. Oh well, it was definitely fun while it lasted.

I grab a few things from the cupboards too. My favorite herbal tea and some cookies. A packet of granola and some packets of soup. I feel weird about doing a big shop at the boys' place. Matty was pretty clear that he expected me to make myself at home, but I'm not going to be the house guest who's found with their feet up on the designer coffee table. I'm going to try and make sure I make as little impact as possible on their home.

While I wait for another cab, I message my friend Hope to tell her I'm back. She calls me the second it's delivered.

"What do you mean you came back early?" she shouts. "You were on vacation. What could possibly have been so important you had to leave vacation?"

"Hello to you too!" I laugh. "It wasn't something important, it was something unpleasant."

"Oh no. Not your mom again?"

I laugh again because she knows without me even saying anything. That's how bad my mom's reputation is for her behavior.

"She's getting married, Hope."

"Married. Who the hell would be prepared to put up with that for better and for worse? Don't they realize it's likely to mostly be for worse?"

"He's not that different from her. I think they might be a match made in hell."

Hope chuckles. "So you're angry that she's getting married? I'd have thought you'd be happy that she'd have something else to focus her laser sharp tongue on."

"Nah. It's not that. To be honest, I'm happy that she's found someone that can take away some of her focus from me. It's complicated. Seems I'm going to be getting a bigger family."

"Hell-dude has kids?"

"Four grown sons."

"Stepbrothers," she squeals. "You're gonna have four stepbrothers. I'm so jealous!"

"My life isn't one of your romance novels, you know."

She huffs as though I've offended her but I know she's laughing inside. I think Hope has one of the biggest Kindle collections of Stepbrother Romance Novels of anyone in the world. She's always had a thing for them, ever since our other friend Jenna found herself living with the sexiest stepbrother in the world. OMG. If Jenna hadn't snapped Harrison up, I'd have been worried for his health. Hope had serious plans for that guy.

"You wish it was," she said. "If every guy was like one of my book boyfriends, all women would be walking around with smiles on their faces and divorce lawyers would all be going out of business."

"Maybe," I laugh.

"So did you meet them?"

"Yeah,"

"And you didn't like them?

I think about the moment I laid eyes on Callum and Liam; the impact their presence had on me was mind-blowing. And Ryan and Matty too. How the hell am I going to explain it all?

"Mom was rude to me in front of them and I was so angry I just wanted to come home."

"Oh for fuck sake," Hope says with all the passion that only a best friend can have in support of you. "What the hell is that woman's problem? I know she's your mom, but she's just too much and it's not okay for her to keep hurting you all the time."

"I know. And thanks, sweetie. I'm okay now that I'm back."

"So are you just gonna hang out at home until she comes back and lays into you again?"

"Nah…I've kinda got somewhere else to stay."

"Where?" she asks, intrigued. "You managed to find alternative accommodation pretty quickly."

"My new stepbrothers offered me their place while I get my life sorted out."

I don't miss the fact that she's gone quiet, and I've known Hope long enough to know what she's doing right now. She's getting lots of puzzle pieces of information from this conversation, sorting them out and placing them into a pattern that will tell her what's been going on. I know I won't need to tell her a thing. She's gonna work it all out just like she always does.

"You had a fling on vacation, didn't you? With one of the brothers. That's why you're playing house-guest."

Hope is like a friggin' mind reader. "I might have had a little fling."

"Little? That doesn't sound very promising. You gonna tell me about it or am I gonna have to trawl the city to find your ass so I can extract the juicy details?"

"Well, it was kinda with two of them." I wait for the sounds of an explosion to happen over the phone because I know I blew her mind. There's silence for a few seconds while my bomb drops, then Hope is back.

"WHAAAAAAAAAT," she screeches. "There is no way you're telling me you had a threesome with your stepbrothers! I know you, Bethany Blane, and…"

I cut her off before she goes off on one completely. "It happened the night of the wedding. They were Dean's best men. Twins."

"TWINNNNNNNS," she screeches. "You…I can't believe you're living out my favorite book!"

"Which one's that?" I ask.

She scoffs. "You totally don't need to ask that question, girl. So what was it like…tell me it was amazing…tell me it was all my dreams and fantasies rolled into one."

"It was," I say softly.

"Oh my god. You are so damn lucky. And you left all that behind because of your mom. You're crazy, girl. Crazy."

"I think I might be," I say.

A horn blasts outside. My cab is waiting at the curb. "I'm gonna have to go, Hope," I say. "I'll text you my new address. I'll be around if you're free?"

"I can't believe you're leaving me hanging like this!" she says in such an exasperated voice that I burst out laughing.

"Listen, girl, you've read enough stepbrother ménage novels to be able to guess at some of what happened. My cab's outside. I'll fill you in another time. Byeeee!"

I hang up before she can say anything else, just to make her a little madder! Talking to my bestie has definitely cheered me up.

I haul my things outside and the cab driver loads the bags into the trunk. Just as I'm about to get in the car my phone rings again. The first thing to cross my mind is that it's Hope calling back, desperate for all the juicy details. That girl has no patience.

Then I see Brad's name flash up on the screen and feel sick to my stomach in a flash. What the hell? When I walked out, he swore he'd never speak to me again. The loss of control over me was too much for him to take. When I wasn't malleable anymore he wasn't interested, and because I'd defied and humiliated him, he needed to at least try and reject me too.

I have no idea what he's calling about and I don't want to pick up either, but I know if I don't and he doesn't leave a message the curiosity will bug me. Add to that the pressure that he'll be expecting me to call him back and worse that he could call back at any time! It seems the best option to pick up and try to sound unaffected. The truth is that even though I am more than over him, I still get trembles in my hands and an anxious feeling in my chest. I hate it, but I just don't know what I can do about it. Maybe it won't ever change.

"Hello."

"Bethany," he says in his most charming tone, and I feel another wave of nausea. "Long time no speak."

"Has it been?"

He's quiet momentarily and I know he won't like me questioning him. I hear him inhale and can sense that he's trying to keep calm. "Well, I suppose it hasn't been that long. Anyway, I was wondering if you could come over and collect the things that you've left here."

I frown because I was sure I had taken everything when I left. I guess I must not have been as thorough as I thought I was. "What did you find?"

"Well, there are some photos and some other small personal effects. I didn't want to throw them away in case they were things you wanted." I inwardly curse myself for failing to take things that sound like they might be important to me. At this point, I'd get him to throw away pretty much anything to avoid having to be in his company again, but not photos. Photos are precious moments and I don't want to forget any of those.

As much as it pains me to arrange to see him, I guess I have to. "I'm in a cab. I could shoot by now."

He's silent for a second. I don't think he was expecting me to suggest right now. "That'll be fine, I suppose."

"I'll be around twenty minutes with traffic."

"Okay then. I'll see you then."

I hang up feeling dirty. Everything about his tone and manner makes my skin crawl, but I'll be okay with the cab driver waiting for me. I'll be in and out of there as fast as I can with as little conversation as I can manage.

This day just keeps getting stranger and stranger. One minute I'm on vacation, the next I'm heading to see an ex who I want to keep firmly in the past.

I tell the driver the new address and he adjusts his route to get there as quickly as possible. All the way, I'm fidgeting. Just going back to his apartment is hard. When I think back to the memories of the time we spent together, there are so few pleasant moments to recollect. It's all days tinged with sadness or anger, depending on how Brad was behaving. If he was in a bad mood, then he'd want to bring me down. If he was in a good mood then often he'd want to undermine me, just to make himself feel even better. It was like a pendulum swinging from misery to more misery until I lost myself in his criticism. It took too long for me to realize what was happening, and even when I'd admitted it to myself, I felt ashamed to confess it to the world.

To try and relieve my anxiety, I message Hope the address of Liam's place and tell her that I'll definitely share all the juicy details next time I see her. I get some angry red-faced emoji's back that make me chuckle.

The driver turns slowly into the lot and I look up to where Brad's windows are. I can almost feel his eyes on the cab and a shudder runs through me. I take three deep breaths then square my shoulders and open the car door. I tell the driver to wait for me, and then I'm off to go and retrieve my final things.

This is absolutely the last time I'm going to see Brad. I make a promise to myself. It's not because I'm too weak to face him, or too beaten down. It's because, no matter how much time passes, he will still be the same cruel and evil fucker and I will still know. I can't forget how he treated me. I can't forget the malice in his eyes or the glee I witnessed when he really got me to crumble. Brad will never be a good person, no matter how much he puts a front on for the world, and I just don't want to put myself through being around him anymore!

The ride in the elevator is painful. My hands are trembling so I clasp them together. I can feel sweat in the small of my back. Primal reactions to deep emotional damage. The hate I feel for him is so sharp it's like a blade inside me. There are times when I've imagined how I'd feel if he died and I know it would be joy. As a person with a strong moral compass, that realization is uncomfortable, but I can't do anything to change it.

The elevator doors open and I see his door at the end of the corridor. It's number 13 and that always made it feel a little creepy. I linger in the elevator with my hand over the sensor, debating what to do next. I've come this far but I could back out. I could let the doors close and be done with it. I could leave my photos and the precious memories they may hold and accept the loss, but I can't. I don't want to let him steal anything more from me than he already has.

I walk down the hall slowly but once I'm at the door I knock with purpose. My heart skips quadruple time while I wait for Brad to open up. I can hear him walking around inside and I take a step back to put some distance between where I'm standing and where he'll be when he comes to the door. There's a familiar sound as he unlocks; one that used to fill me with dread when he'd come home from work. I turn to look down the corridor as if my body is frantically considering escape. Fight or flight and I'm definitely tempted to do the latter.

Then he whips the door open and I'm frozen like a rabbit in headlights.

I used to think Brad was gorgeous. I used to feel unworthy of being in a relationship with him. I saw how other girls would gaze at him when we were out, but the more I got to see who he was inside, the more like a gargoyle he appeared. Now I see the darkness within him marring his face like a twisted mask. His eyes aren't smoldering anymore, they're sinister and frightening.

"Bethany," he says with a fake smile and a drawl that anyone who was listening would think was soft with affection. I know the truth, though.

"Where are the things?" I say, trying to keep my voice even. I reach into my pocket and finger my phone, not wanting to hold his gaze.

"They're just here," he says. His arm waves in the direction of the table in the hallway. "Would you like to come in?"

"No thanks. I'll just take them."

"You're just going to stand in the hallway?" he asks with a smug edge to his voice, as though he knows I'm scared and is reveling in it. "I think you should come in and see the photos."

"I really don't need to," I tell him. "I have a cab outside. I'll just take them and go, okay?"

His eyes flash bright with something that looks a lot like glee. "Okay. If you want to."

He leaves me at the door and goes to get a small brown bag from the console table, then returns, holding it out to me as though it contains something foul smelling.

"Thanks," I say, taking the handle, but he doesn't let go.

"You know, Bethany, you really made a big mistake walking out of here." I tug at the bag, now desperate to get away, but he holds firm. "You thought you could just leave me and there would be no consequences." Brad leans forward, his nostrils flaring, and I let go of the bag, taking two steps back. He looks seriously fucking angry and for a second I think he's going to hit me, but he doesn't.

Instead, he takes a deep breath, straightens his posture, and drops the bag on the floor.

"Take your things and get out of here," he hisses, then turns and slams the door.

My heart is beating so fast I can't think what to do. The bag sits on the floor two feet in front of me but I can't bring myself to walk closer to the apartment. I look over my shoulder, hoping there will be someone coming up in the elevator but the hallway is empty. Brad's door is still closed and with my eyes fixed firmly on it, I grab out for the bag and hurry away. I don't want to run because he's probably looking at me through the spy hole like the deranged freak that he is, but I'm practically jogging. The elevator has returned to the ground floor so I opt to take the stairs, sprinting down them as fast as I can. The brown bag rustles, brushing against my leg but I don't look inside it. I can't. Not until I know I'm safely away.

The cab driver is parked where he left me, and the relief I feel when I get back into the car and slam the door is so great that tears spring to my eyes. I take so many deep breaths that I begin to feel woozy.

"Are you okay, Miss?" the driver looks over his shoulder.

"Can we get out of here?" I say quietly, just about holding myself together.

"Sure thing." He pulls away and I don't think I've ever been so happy to leave anywhere in my life.

The brown bag rests on my knee and I look at it, hoping that whatever is contained inside was worth the awful stress that I just went through. I open it up, finding a lipstick, a couple of pens with my business logo on them, and a CD that was probably in Brad's car. There's an envelope too. I pull it out and open the flap, feeling confused. I've never been to this photo developer before. Maybe he just used one of his envelopes to stash my pictures? I don't recognize the top photo. It's a close up of me in black and white. I look preoccupied and am wearing way more makeup than usual. I flick to the next picture and Kerry's with me, her hair fixed up elaborately. I look closer.

It's at the wedding. These pictures were taken a few days ago.

How the fuck did he get pictures of the wedding?

My heart starts to thump harder again. Has he been stalking me? Was he watching me at the wedding? My hands fumble as I shuffle through the photos. There's some of me with the twins at the reception when we were standing at the bar. They're taken from an odd angle so you can't see much, but I know what's coming now. I don't have to look any further to know he has pictures of me with the twins, but I do. Like a robot, I gaze at picture after picture of me in more and more compromising positions, and I feel sick. Absolutely sick to my stomach.

But it gets worse. Scrawled across the last picture, in Brad's jagged handwriting, are some words that cut me to the core. 'I always knew you were a whore, but now everyone else will too."

And suddenly my world falls apart.

16
KNIGHTS IN WHITE T-SHIRTS

I'm a trembling mess by the time the cab drops me off in front of the O'Connell brothers' building. The driver unloads my bags and I stand on the curb feeling lost. I don't know who to turn to for help. I can't burden Kerry with all this. There is no way I can tell mom. I'm assuming that Brad is planning to show the photos to my loved ones and ruin my reputation. Maybe he's thinking he could ruin my business with those pictures too. Maybe he'd be right.

Who would want to buy their kids birthday cake from a woman who indulges in dubious sexual practices? It's not that my clientele are particularly religious or traditional or anything, but I know how I felt about the idea of group sex before I indulged in it and I'm by no means a prude.

I am a private person though. I kept my terrible life with Brad a secret from everyone. Even now, only Kerry and Hope know the true extent of the emotional abuse I suffered. Mom thinks I'm the most foolish woman in the world for leaving Prince Charming behind. Little does she know he was really the wolf.

Now my privacy could be permanently taken from me. I know what happens when photos are leaked. You can never remove them all. Images spread across the internet like wildfire. People share social media posts that are hot gossip. My life will never be the same if Brad tries to ruin me.

I look over my shoulder at the apartment block that I'm supposed to be staying in and realize that going in there could make it all worse. What if Brad is still having me tailed and I'm photographed moving luggage here? Talk about adding fuel to the fire. But where else can I go?

I think about calling Hope, but she's still living with her parents and I certainly don't want to be bringing drama of this kind to her doorstep.

My mind isn't functioning properly. I still have the pictures in my trembling hands. I don't want to look at them again but I can't bring myself to put them away in my purse. Anything that has come from Brad feels like poison. I can almost feel the negative energy coming from these photographs; the hatred he must have felt when he saw them, and the sense of wicked enjoyment I could tell he was getting from handing them over to me and putting himself back in control again.

It all makes me feel sick to my stomach.

I don't know what to do.

A car pulls up a little way down the curb and I look up, noticing it's another cab. I look away when the doors open and stare up the road in the other direction, my mind still whirring through options but coming up with nothing. Then I hear my name.

I know it's Ryan before I even look. There's something so distinct about his voice. That steely determination and cockiness that got on my nerves so much in Jamaica. I turn, to find him striding toward me.

"Hey," he says. "Didn't expect to find you out here looking like an orphan."

I blink, tears burning the back of my throat like razors. I can't bring myself to speak because I know I'll break down if I do.

Behind Ryan, Matty is sorting out the bill with the cab driver and retrieving their suitcases. Just seeing them here makes me feel so much better.

Safe.

Protected.

Foolish.

I'm so stupid to feel this way. These men don't owe me anything. This is just a fucked up situation and for whatever reason fate seems to have put us on the same journey for now.

"Are you okay?" Ryan asks, putting his hand on my upper arm in a way that is so sweet and reassuring. For all his gruffness, I can sense that his concern is sincere.

I shake my head and he doesn't hesitate. One second I'm standing alone and bereft, the next I'm in Ryan's embrace, and it feels so good. "Hey." He strokes my hair gently and shushes me as I start to cry. It's not just the fear I'm feeling now that's driving my emotion. It's the years of soul-destroying loneliness I felt with Brad and the shattered feeling in my heart. It's the shame of never living up to my mom's expectations, of being a disappointment to everyone.

I think Ryan understands that I'm past consoling on the street. He scoops me into his arms as though I weigh nothing and starts toward the lobby. "It's okay, Bethany. We're here and we're gonna get you inside."

I hear the sound of luggage dragging and assume that Matty is following. I can't worry about anything though, because I just can't stop crying. It's as though now that the dam has burst, the tears just won't stop flowing. Ryan holds me tight all the way in the elevator and even manages to open the door without putting me down. I'm so mortified but that doesn't stop me from burying my face in his chest and soaking up his strength. He feels like Liam and Callum and he smells like them too, but it's more than that. Ryan is strong and capable. He's fierce and no nonsense. He's everything I need right now.

He sits on the sofa with me still clinging to him like a baby monkey. I hear Matty coming up the corridor with the bags, then the click of the door. Seconds later he's next to us and his warm hand is on my shoulder.

"Bethany," he says gently. "Tell us what's wrong."

I shake my head. I'm still clutching the packet of photos though. The easiest thing to do would be to pass them over. It's not like the subject matter is going to be a surprise to them. They got to see plenty that the photographer's lens didn't reach. I know they won't be expecting to see photographic evidence of it, though.

Matty takes the envelope from me and begins to shuffle through the pictures. I know the moment he's realized what they are when he swears under his breath.

"What are they?" Ryan asks.

"Photos of Bethany with Liam and Callum, and a threat to expose them."

I feel Ryan's anger in the way his body goes rigid and his grip on me intensifies. "Who gave you those, Bethany?" he asks. His voice is as tight as his grip, and I understand. His brothers are threatened too.

"My ex," I say.

"How did he give them to you?"

"He asked me to go to his place to pick up a few things I left behind when I walked out."

"Did he threaten you?" Ryan's voice is a hiss now. A seriously pissed-off hiss.

"Not when I was there. He left the note to do that."

I know the twins are looking at each other trying to work out what the fuck is going on.

"Bethany, do you have a bad history with this guy?"

I nod and Ryan swears under his breath. He adjusts his hold on me so he can tip my face up and look into my eyes. I must look like a complete mess after all that sobbing; red puffy eyes and runny nose. I don't want him to see me like this or know my history, but it seems that I'm not going to get a choice in either.

"He never hit me but he was mentally abusive and controlling," I say.

"Are you scared of him?" Matty asks. I nod my head because it's the truth. He may not be violent, but the cool calculation behind his words and his actions make me worried for his potential to harm me in indirect ways. Even though I'm not with him anymore, I still carry that fear. I don't know if the paranoia will ever go away.

"Why the fuck did you go over there then?" Ryan growls. "You should have stayed far away. Tell him to mail your stuff or wait until you had someone to go with you."

"I don't want him to know I'm scared. He feeds off that. I thought I was better. Since I've been away from him I've been feeling better."

"But you're not, are you?" Matty brushes my damp hair away from my forehead tenderly.

I shake my head and bury my face against Ryan again. His arms fold tightly around me as though he wishes he could shield me from all the horrors in the world. I wish he could too.

"He's not going to get away with this shit, Bethany," Ryan mutters. "Do you hear me?"

I nod, but even though part of me is glad he's mad and wants to do something about it, another part of me is scared. I have no idea how far Brad will go to seek revenge for his humiliation. I don't want the boys to get dragged into something because of me.

"We need to call Liam and Callum," Matty says.

I shake my head. "Don't tell them," I say. "This is all my fault. I don't want them getting dragged into this."

"They're in the pictures too, Bethany. They're about as far into this as they can get. And if these pictures get out it could be bad for business. They'd want to know. Let's just call it damage control."

Matty gets up to go and make the call and I use the distraction to disentangle myself from Ryan, feeling totally embarrassed. Of course they're worried about the impact to their brothers. There was me thinking that Matty and Ryan were worried about me and wanting to protect me. I'm just a third party here. The cause but not the concern.

I move quickly into Liam's room and head straight for the bathroom, locking the door. My chest hurts, my eyes are sore and I feel totally wrung out. The me that looks back from the mirror is a wreck. All the color in my cheeks from my days in the sun has washed away and the girl who is standing here now looks like me after Brad. Those dark days when I first moved back home are ones I'd rather forget, but it seems that I can't.

He won't let me.

He's going to keep dragging me back in.

I splash water on my face and dry it on a ridiculously soft towel. I try to smooth my hair but it needs a brush and there doesn't seem to be one to hand. It's never easy to be upset and be away from your home space. It's at times like this when curling up on your own bed and hiding from the world seems like the best possible thing to do. I don't have that luxury, but, as I make my way back into Liam's room, his bed looks so appealing. I slip off my shoes and pull back the comforter. It's such a comfortable bed and, under the covers, I feel protected from everything that is going on outside of these four walls. I'm expecting Ryan or Matty to come and find me. I'm expecting them to tell me I need to get up and deal with Brad and his bullshit, but it doesn't happen.

I'm so exhausted that I close my eyes.

I hear voices and footsteps as the twins move around the house. I have no idea what they're planning outside of telling Callum and Liam, and what that will mean is anyone's guess. I don't know them well enough to know how they'll react to such an intrusion into their privacy. As much as Brad's actions are designed to hurt me, they have just as much power to hurt the twins as well. My heart aches for it. My frivolous actions have caused so many issues for so many people.

I should never have tried to break free from the confines of my life. I should have known that happiness and excitement were not things I could expect for myself.

Tears well in my eyes again and I swipe at them, embarrassed that I have so little control over my emotions and angry that I just can't seem to get a grip. I'm not a teenager anymore. These kinds of dramas were supposed to end after high school and college. Everything is still getting on top of me and I just feel like I'm failing.

There's a soft knock at the door and I wipe my face again before calling out that it's okay for whoever is out there to come in.

Ryan opens the door wide and comes straight over to the bed without hesitation. He's carrying a glass of water and I sit up and take a long drink, so grateful for his thoughtfulness.

"We spoke to Liam and Callum," he says.

I cringe, imagining the kind of reaction they might have had. Were they angry at me? The thought hurts my heart. "What did they say?" I ask, not really sure I want to know the answer.

"I won't repeat the exact words." Ryan smirks and sits on the edge of the bed. "Can you give me as many details as you have about this ex of yours? I'm going to need full name, birth date, address, place of work, the car he drives…basically anything you can think of that will help us deal with him."

"What are you planning to do?" As much as I want Brad to fry for what he's put me through and is intending to do, the thought that the O'Connell brothers might do something outside the law scares me.

"You don't need to worry about anything, Bethany. Let us take care of this asshole now."

"I don't want you to do anything that'll get you into trouble. You don't know what he's capable of."

"Seriously, Bethany. Any guy who gets his kicks from threatening women is one that needs to get taken down, and believe me, we're not going to do something that'll risk anything important."

"But you don't understand. He's not going to let this go. I humiliated him by leaving and now he wants to hurt me. He's not going to stop until he gets his revenge."

"Oh, he will," Ryan says and the fierceness that darkens his eyes has me believing that he might just be capable of what he's promising. A selfish part of me would love to see Ryan beat the living daylights out of Brad, but that would only end badly for Ryan.

Ryan grabs a notepad from Liam's desk and I relay all the information he's asked for.

"Just promise me that you'll be careful," I say when we're done.

Ryan leans forward and tucks a stray strand of hair behind my ear. He smiles. "You know what, Bethany? If I didn't know you better, I'd think you cared."

I flush at his words and the heat in his eyes. Ryan succeeded in making the worst first impression on me, and the way he came across at the beach sealed my feelings about him firmly into the negative. Now, though, I'm not so sure. He's so tough and abrasive. He doesn't hide his thoughts or feelings and he certainly doesn't mince his words, and all of that should be really unappealing, except I can see now that it comes from a good place. He's brutally honest because that's what he seeks from other people. He's fiercely protective of the ones he loves. I think back to that beach conversation and suddenly see things from a different perspective. He was worried about his brothers and thought I was jerking them around.

I can't even guess at what he thinks now, but I find that I care. I want him to know that I'm a good person and that I don't take other people's feelings for granted. I want him to know that I never set out to use anyone or hurt anyone. To be honest, I thought the twins were just up for some vacation fun. I still think that's the case deep down. It's just Ryan and Matty who seem convinced that they had something else in mind.

"I do care, Ryan," I tell him. "I really wish that none of this was happening."

"Do you wish you never hooked up with my brothers?" he asks, cocking his head to one side.

I shake my head and look at my hands that are resting on top of Liam's gorgeous comforter. "I regret what is happening now…what could happen to them because of what we did together, but I don't regret what we did. Your brothers are amazing men and they treated me with nothing but kindness and respect."

Ryan smiles. "That's good," he says. "You know, me and Matty are amazing too."

I smile and he reaches out to touch my cheek, brushing his thumb over the corner of my mouth.

"You have the prettiest smile," he says. "Even when you're sad."

"I'm not sad," I tell him. "Just worried and tired. I just wish that things could be easier."

"Things will be easier, Bethany. Don't you worry about that. We'll do everything in our power to make things better for you."

I look into his liquid gray eyes and some of the warmth I see there seeps into my heart.

"You should get some sleep and we'll talk again in the morning," he says softly and I nod.

I look down at myself, still in the clothes I traveled back in from Jamaica. Then I realize I have no idea why Ryan and Matty aren't still on vacation.

"How come you came back early too?" I ask.

"We got a call about a problem with one of our biggest contracts. Matty is trying to sort out a solution right now. We're may need to fly to Mexico City tomorrow or the day after, depending on the outcome. I'm hoping we'll be able to get it resolved though."

"Oh," I say, feeling despondent. Now that they're here, I really don't want them to leave again.

Ryan grins again as though he can read my mind. "Get some z's in, baby girl. We're gonna have a busy day tomorrow."

As he walks away I can't stop myself from admiring how strong and masculine he looks. For all my worry and anxiety, a part of me thinks that maybe it'll be a good thing if Ryan and Matty leave town again soon because I'm starting to feel very muddled about the younger twins too.

Giving in to one set of twins has already gotten me into enough trouble.

Desiring their younger twin brothers is just foolish icing on the cake.

17

A SISTERLY AWAKENING

For someone who never sleeps well in strange beds, I'm shocked to find that I wake up late after a solid night of sleep in Liam's. It's so comfortable I feel like I slept in a cloud. I'm so content that it takes a couple of seconds of blurriness for me to remember what happened the day before.

Brad.

Ryan and Matty are back.

Callum and Liam know that they're in the pictures.

My empty stomach rolls at the thought of what I might have to face today. Brad may have already made good on his threats. Whatever Ryan and Matty were hoping to do to stop him from releasing those photos may be too late.

I swing my legs over the side of the bed and look down at my crumpled clothes. Someone brought the rest of my belongings into the room while I was sleeping so I search for something clean to wear and head to the bathroom to freshen up.

When I'm done, I nervously open the door, unsure of what I'm going to find on the other side. Will Ryan be angry? Will they be leaving soon? I just hate all the uncertainty.

The twins are both in the kitchen, sitting at the counter with steaming mugs of coffee and empty plates in front of them. Ryan is the first to look up and he nods and smiles.

"Looks like sleeping beauty is up," he says. Matty looks up from his phone and smiles too, then his expression changes.

"Why so serious, Bethany?" he asks.

I frown because surely he should know why I'm feeling worried. "The photos," I say, clasping my hands together nervously.

Matty gets down from his stool and strides to where I'm standing. He puts his hands on my upper arms and squeezes reassuringly. His eyes are so soft and beautiful as he smiles. "Do you trust us?" he asks. It doesn't take me any time to nod because I do. Even though we haven't known each other for long, I have so much faith in these men to do the right thing.

"Then you let us deal with this bullshit."

He cups my cheek as I nod, and for a second I forget that it's Matty in front of me. His actions are like Callum's and Liam's. The intensity of his gaze and the touch of his hand against my skin feels familiar. I close my eyes because there are too many emotions bubbling inside me.

As much as I don't want to admit it to myself, I miss the twins a lot. I'm so worried about what Brad is capable of and how it could affect us all. I'm concerned that Ryan and Matty are going to take on something that will explode in their faces and I don't want them to be hurt in any way.

Most of all I just feel lonely and I hate myself for it. I never wanted to be the kind of woman who was needy, but I guess I am. My body craves affection and comfort in a way that I'm ashamed of because I'm all grown up and I should be able to stand on my own two feet.

I expect Matty to pull away so I can busy myself making coffee and breakfast and pretend that everything is fine. Then I feel a soft brush on my lips and I open my eyes with a start.

It felt like a kiss but it wasn't. It was something almost more erotic. Matty brushed his thumb across my lips and my heart skipped. He's looking at me with half-closed eyes and I know my pupils must be blown wide because I realize now that I want him to kiss me.

His chin has a days'-worth of scruff and his cheeks are a little burned by the sun. Matty looks rugged, but his eyes and hands are kind. The perfect combination.

"Bethany," he says softly, tucking my hair behind my ears. "I want to kiss you so badly, but it's not the time."

I blink because I didn't expect him to come out and say it. Being blatant is Ryan's forte, but it seems like these younger twins have a little more in common than I thought.

"I think she wants to kiss you too," Ryan says. When I look at him he's smiling knowingly. The Cheshire Cat. I should be angry at his smugness, but how can I be when he's only saying what is patently obvious.

HUGE X4

The only thing on my mind is how Callum and Liam would feel if they could see me now.

"Your brothers…" I say, looking at the ground in shame.

"…are on a flight here," Ryan says.

I look up with shock. "I thought they were going back to Dubai."

"They have a few more days of vacation but couldn't just sit on a beach in Jamaica when all of this is going on over here."

"I…" I take a step back from Matty. I can't believe what was close to happening and how stupid I was about to be.

"I know what you're thinking, and you don't need to go there," Matty says. "We're not territorial about that kind of thing."

I open my mouth to reply but I'm not sure what to say.

I think that he just referred to me as territory. That feels a little mortifying.

I should be upset at the idea that Callum and Liam would be so blasé about sharing me with their brothers. I should be, but this is hardly a normal situation where normal standards of behavior apply, is it?

I find myself thinking that it's nice that these brothers are so in tune with each other. Siblings can be competitive and I don't get the feeling that the O'Connell brothers are at all. Then I feel ridiculous for being so fluffy about something I should be taking more seriously.

Ryan chuckles from his side of the counter. "I think you've broken her brain." He stands, picking up his mug and plate and walking them to the sink. "Callum and Liam are going to get a taxi from the airport while we deal with the current situation. Will you be here when they arrive?"

I nod because right now I've got nothing to do and nowhere to go. I should still be in Jamaica sunning myself and relaxing. Instead, I'm here, stressing and feeling a lot like a fish out of water.

"That's good," Matty says.

Ryan comes closer, his eyes softer than I've ever seen them. "You don't need to worry about anything, baby girl," he says, cupping my cheek. I want to nuzzle into his hand, like an affection-starved cat but I resist. "We're gonna take care of your douchebag ex and be back in time for lunch. Then he does something that I'm not expecting. He leans in and kisses my lips so gently it's like a whisper. My heart skips fast because it feels so right but I know it's wrong.

All of this is wrong.

And it gets even more inappropriate when Ryan steps back and Matty does the same thing. I've closed my eyes by this point so I don't have to look at them. I know they'll see the truth right there; that I like what they're doing and I want it. Oh, I'm a terrible person. A deeply sinful person.

And the O'Connell brothers are my temptation.

All four of them.

It feels so wrong I'm almost expecting to get struck down from above. Then Ryan slaps my ass and they both chuckle, and I'm left standing in the kitchen feeling like a total idiot while they head to their rooms.

I'm not even hungry. How could I be at a time like this?

HUGE X4

I fix myself a glass of water and head back to Liam's room to hide out. The front door goes a little while later when I'm in the middle of checking my emails. There are some new orders that I schedule in for next week and then send some confirmation responses. Business doesn't stop for life drama.

I make a call to my accountant to confirm some boring financial stuff. Then my phone rings.

I look down at the screen nervously; almost expecting it to be Brad, but it's my sister.

"Oh my god, Bethany," she says when I pick up. "I was so worried about you."

"I'm sorry, sis," I say. There is no way I want her to be wasting her honeymoon concerned about me, but I'm not surprised. Leaving like that without telling her wasn't fair. "I should have called you to tell you I was getting a flight out, but you were busy and I didn't want to disturb."

"Oh my god. You can disturb me anytime…you know that." She sounds exasperated.

"I know…but that doesn't mean I think I should."

"So what the hell happened that had you running away?"

"Mom," I say and Kerry sighs.

"That woman just doesn't get any easier with age."

I chuckle even though it's not really a laughing matter and I'm in no way feeling in a humorous mood. It's what Kerry will be expecting me to do and I don't want her to get a whiff of anything else going on here.

"So what did she do?" Kerry asks.

"She didn't tell you?"

"No. Just said you'd gone home early."

"She humiliated me in front of our soon-to-be-stepbrothers."

There's a pause. "Rewind a second," she says. "Stepbrothers?" There's another pause as I realize that Kerry has no idea about mom's wedding plans.

"You mean mom didn't tell you?"

"I don't know what you're talking about," Kerry says.

"Mom's getting married," I say chuckling nervously. "And let's just say I think she's found the perfect match."

"Married?" she splutters.

"Err yeah. To Liam and Callum's father, Frank O'Connell."

"What?!"

I hear Dean's voice in the background and then Kerry fills him in. I hear him say 'what the fuck' before Kerry comes back on the line.

"So you left because you're unhappy about the situation or because mom was her usual self?"

I pause because I would usually tell my sister everything but I'm not sure what to say on this occasion. Especially because Dean is sitting right next to her and it concerns his friends. I mean, he probably already knows what they get up to but knowing they did that with me is a bit more than I want to share with my new brother-in-law.

"I'm not unhappy she's getting married. I'm not even unhappy she's marrying a man that I think is a bit of an ass because he'll suit her perfectly. I'm totally embarrassed about the way she spoke to me in front of practical strangers."

"But you didn't have to leave because of that. The twins won't care about something like that."

"I know they won't…it's just…"

I pause because I've got no idea how to explain without confessing it all. It's not that I'm worried that Kerry will be shocked or think badly of me. We have friends who are happy in polyamorous relationships. Very happy. It's more that I'm struggling to piece it all together in my own mind, let alone be able to articulate it to someone else.

I certainly don't want to tell her while she's sitting next to Dean. Men talk just as much as women! Maybe now's not the time, but then again, if I don't tell her she's likely to be pissed at me when she eventually finds out. I decide to bite the bullet.

"Kerry," I say. "Can you move away from Dean a little so I can tell you something?"

"Sure." She sounds intrigued. "Just gonna get a bottle of water," she tells him. "Do you want anything?" I hear mumbling in the background and then the sound of her moving. "I'm heading up to the bar," she tells me. "Spit it out then!"

"I did something kinda bad," I say.

"I knew it," she squeals and then proceeds to giggle. "Those boys couldn't keep their eyes off you at the reception, and I know all about what they're like from Dean…" She pauses. "You did do what I think you did."

"Yes," I say in a small voice.

"Oh my god…good for you, Bethany!"

I exhale a long breath, feeling so relieved that she's reacted how I hoped she would. Kerry knows how hard I've had it and how much of a huge step it was for me to go there with Liam and Callum. "It was pretty amazing," I say. "They are amazing."

"So why the hell did you leave?"

"Because they're going to be our stepbrothers, Kerry. And their dad was really angry about it."

"He knows?" she gasps.

"I guess their preferences aren't a secret," I say, blushing.

"Seems like their preference is you, sis." She giggles. "Damn girl, you really know how to upstage a woman on her wedding night!"

I laugh. "I'm sure Dean did what he needed to do."

"You have no idea," Kerry replies dreamily. "But let's not talk about the boring marrieds. Let's talk about the hot sex with twin stepbrothers."

"That's the problem, though. As hot as it was, it can't happen again. And the fact that Frank knows about it probably means that mom knows too. How am I ever going to be in the same room with them all?"

"Listen, Bethany. You're not related to them. You're not married. You hadn't taken a vow of chastity. Can you just chill out for a second? Anyone who thinks badly of you for having some enjoyable adult time as a single woman just isn't worth bothering about."

"Including mom?"

"Especially mom. You know what, Bethany. We've pretended to all get along for such a long time. We've ignored her controlling personality and her abrasive way of communicating, but to be really honest, I'm done. Dean hates seeing me upset by her. If I don't pull away a little, they're going to end up coming to blows. I think you need to think about doing the same thing. Move out of that house. Get your own place. See her out in public so she'll have a little thought about making sure her behavior is suitable for an audience, and live your life in a way that is going to make you happy."

"You really think that?" I ask, shocked that this is how she feels. For as long as I can remember it has been mostly me with the issue with mom, or so I thought. Kerry has a way of smiling through difficult situations that made me think she wasn't as affected. I guess I was wrong.

"Yeah, I do. Life is short, sis. And you've had a particularly shitty time recently. If you like Liam and Callum and they make you feel good, then what's the harm in enjoying it?"

I think about the potential catastrophe that could be about to detonate if Brad gets his way. I can't tell Kerry about that. She'll be on a plane home before I can finish the conversation. There's no way I'm ruining her honeymoon.

She needs to know where I am, though. "So, I guess I should tell you that Matty, their brother, offered to let me crash at their apartment so I don't have to be in mom's company. That's where I'm calling from."

"You're in their apartment," she says. "Now?"

"Yeah. It's gorgeous."

"And you're going to stay there?"

"Just until I can find a place for myself or it gets too uncomfortable."

"Wow," she says. "Talk about throwing yourself in the path of temptation."

I laugh again. "Tell me about it. How did one family snag so many great genes? I mean, it's hard to look at them, they are all so gorgeous."

"Do you think they…" She giggles as though she's embarrassed to even say the next bit. "Do you think they all share?"

"I think there is a pretty good chance that they do."

"Oh my goodness," Kerry mutters. "That is just too much hotness for a girl to handle." She has no idea how right she is.

"You're a bad influence," I tell her.

She scoffs. "Hardly. Look at me. Boring married for the second time."

"Dean is not boring in any way."

"I know." I can hear the smile in her voice and it makes me smile too. "I don't know how I did it for a second time, but I struck gold with my baby. Anyway, speaking of babies, I really need to get back to Dean. He's gonna be sending out a search party for me in a minute."

"Yeah, get back to your honeymoon, girl. And don't worry about me. I'll muddle through like I always do."

"Give yourself a bit more credit, sweetie. You've made some good and brave decisions recently. Who says that what happened here wasn't one of them."

"All the rational and sensible people in the world," I say, thinking of the photos and cringing.

"Yeah, but they're all dying of boredom in loveless marriages!" We both laugh and it feels good, despite my undercurrent of worry.

"True. Thanks, Kerry. For always making me see the funny side of everything and for telling me that I know what I'm doing, even if I don't really believe it's the case."

"You just gotta trust yourself. Trust your instincts. You know what, Bethany? It's when you doubt yourself that you go wrong. It's when you know that something isn't right in your heart of hearts but you don't want to rock the boat, or you make someone else's issues about you. Believe in your own internal voice and I know you're going to be fine."

Tears spring to my eyes because I think that what Kerry just said is about the nicest thing anyone has ever said to me. My sister believes in me. She believes that I can decide what is right. She believes in me more than I do in myself, but her confidence and faith build mine. A clarity of understanding washes over me.

Brad was the one with issues. He was the one who caused problems in our relationship, who undermined my confidence and made me feel bad for things that were not my fault. He was the one who killed our relationship, not me. If I'd just trusted myself the first time it happened, I would have saved myself so much heartbreak and stopped him from picking at my confidence until he almost unraveled me. If I'd walked away the first time because his behavior had been out of line and beyond what I would have found acceptable for anyone else to put up with, I never would have gone through the soul-crushing experience.

"I love you, Kerry," I say, feeling it overflow my heart in a new way. When you understand that your family and friends see you clearer than you see yourself, it's amazing. When they take the steps to help you see the real you again, it's the best feeling in the world.

"I love you too, sis."

We say our goodbyes and I rest the phone on the comforter, thinking that maybe I should grab myself something to eat before I start to feel funny from a lack of calories.

That's when I hear a key in the door.

18

REVENGE AND REWARD

Callum and Liam are here.

My heart skips like I've been running and my palms feel sweaty because I'm sitting in Liam's room on his bed that I slept in and still haven't made. I look like I've made myself at home and they had no say in the situation at all.

I don't know how I'm going to face them after ignoring them through the hotel room door and skipping town without saying goodbye. They're gonna be mad at me and I don't blame them at all. I'm mad at myself for being cowardly and inconsiderate. I allowed my distress about the way mom treated me to alter the way I treated the twins, and that wasn't good.

I hear them close the front door and pause. Then someone calls my name.

I can't stay hiding in the room forever. I have to face the music, however much I cringe at the thought.

HUGE X4

Footsteps echo on the hardwood floor as I dither over what to do. When I finally find the impetus to stand, I take a quick look in the mirror and smooth my hair. I don't make it any further before they're there, looming large in the doorway.

Two gorgeously tanned, gray-eyed gods wearing the most serious expressions I have ever seen grace their faces. No one says a word but there is so much communicated anyway. I feel a pull between us; a tug that says 'I want to be close to you'. The empty space around me feels emptier now that they're near, as though my body expects for it to be filled. Their eyes are fierce, their posture tense, but it doesn't feel like they're mad at me.

I hope they're not mad at me.

Liam is the first to move, stalking into the room until he's close enough to cup my face in his hands and kiss me. It's a desperate kiss, mirroring exactly how I feel now that they're here. Callum's there too, taking his place behind me, mouth pressed to the top of my head and hands on my hips.

I can't stop myself from reciprocating Liam's kiss or bringing my hand to take hold of one of Callum's. These men feel right where everything else in my life has felt wrong. It shouldn't be the case that they fit with me as they do, but standing pressed between them I feel so safe. Safer than I've ever felt in my life.

I didn't realize just how vulnerable I felt until now. When my dad left he took a big piece of my security with him. I thought that Brad was what I needed because he was strong-willed and dominant, but he didn't want to protect me. His aim was control.

Here in Liam and Callum's arms, I can feel the difference. The passionate need but also desperation to shield me from anything bad.

I tremble because in recognizing this I feel my own vulnerability.

In such a short time these men have taken my battered heart and enclosed it in their big hands. I should be scared. When Kerry told me that I need to start to live again, I was terrified. The idea that I may have to risk my heart again was too much, but here I am and I have no fear that they'll hurt me. Is it odd that I trust them this way?

The only fear I feel is that this won't be a forever space for me. I know the judgment my friends faced when they were open about their polyamorous relationships. Carrie battled with herself for so long before she gave into her stepbrothers. Katelin was fiercer about what she wanted but she had to wait a little for Bryan to fight for her. For all their happiness, they've faced prejudice after prejudice, and I just don't know if I'm strong enough to face it, particularly from my mom. Knowing that Frank was so disapproving distresses me too.

I feel like crying in relief and in dismay. What the hell am I going to do?

Liam pulls back, still holding my face so I can't look away. "You left without saying goodbye." I try to turn but he holds fast. "I wanted to ask if it meant so little to you, but that's stupid because I know that you feel the same, Bethany. I can feel you shaking, Bethany."

Callum strokes my hair and kisses my neck. "When you left we wanted to follow but it didn't seem right to put pressure on you. Then we spoke to Matty and Ryan and we knew we had to come back, regardless of whether you wanted us or not."

There's a hoarseness to his voice that I've never heard before and I turn, finding his face pained. I can't bear to think that he might be hurting because of me. I have to explain so that he understands. "It wasn't that I didn't want you, Callum. Never that. It was because I couldn't see how it was going to ever be what I was starting to want it to be."

"And what's that?" Liam asks.

I turn to face him. "More than a vacation fling," I say nervously, biting my lip. This is a dangerous path of conversation but I need them to understand everything.

"You don't think that we wanted that too?" Callum says fiercely.

"I didn't know, but that's not the point. It's never going to be anything because there are two of you and one of me, and we are going to be stepsiblings. It just can't be, okay."

"Why?" Liam asks. "Because your mom wouldn't like it?"

"And your dad," I say.

"Because they cared so much about our opinions on their relationship!" Callum says. "They got engaged before they told us they were dating for fuck sake."

"And the rest of the world," I say.

"The rest of the world has had some firm opinions on many non-standard relationships in the past, but people have just gotten on with their lives, Bethany. We get to choose how we want to live, don't we?"

"And suffer the consequences," I say.

The twins pause, and I take a step from between them. I need some space to discuss this, so I perch on the end of the bed and look down at my hands.

"I guess you're saying that you're not okay with the consequences," Callum says. He sounds disappointed.

Defeated. I look up and find two sets of gorgeous gray eyes fixed on me. They both look so sad and I can't bear it. "And you can?" I ask.

"We always wanted this," Liam says. He drops to one knee and takes my hand. "Ever since we were teenagers we knew that settling down with separate women just wouldn't work for us. We want to spend our lives together. We want our woman to unite us, not divide us."

"And what about your brothers?" I ask.

"We never thought to hope that far," Callum says softly. "It's always been a long shot that we'd find someone that we want and who'd be willing to live the way we want. To find someone who would accept our brothers too…"

I nod but I don't know what to say.

Fantasy is one thing. A holiday fling that steps totally outside of the bounds of normal relationships was a step far enough for me, but here I am with feelings for all of these brothers. Strong feelings for Liam and Callum, maybe because of the intimacy that we shared and the extra time in each other's company. Just the beginnings of attachment with Ryan and Matty.

They are all so different, but they share common traits of consideration, kindness and protectiveness that I crave so much. Liam and Callum never hoped that they'd find someone who'd accept them all, but if there were no outside concerns, maybe I could. Would I be enough woman for all of them? That's a whole other issue. There are so many questions I want to ask, just to know the answers, but asking them will get their hopes up and I don't think that's fair. The silence feels uncomfortable so I change the subject.

"They've gone to try and sort out the problem," I say, then look to the floor embarrassed.

"We know," Liam says. "Why are you looking like it's your fault, Bethany?"

"Because it is," I say quietly.

"Why? Because you have an ex-boyfriend who is bordering on the pathological?" Callum sounds angry.

"I knew he was angry with me." I pull away from Liam and rest my head in my hands.

"For leaving him?" Liam asks.

I nod. "He wants control over me and now he doesn't have it, he wants to find a way to take it back. He thinks he can use the photos to scare me. While he has them, he can get me to do whatever he wants."

Callum shakes his head. "He doesn't have any power over you that you aren't prepared to give him, baby."

"Callum's right, Bethany. This asshole thinks he can hurt you or hurt us and that you are going to beg him not to. Fuck that."

"What are Ryan and Matty going to do?" I ask.

"We're in the security business. Half our time is spent researching the background of our clients and their contacts. You think that we can't find enough dirt on your ex to make him shit his pants? And if the snake turns out to be clean, then we'll all pay him a visit and let him know who he's dealing with."

"I don't want any of you to get hurt or get in trouble," I say.

"You don't need to worry about any of this, okay."

Callum nods at his brother. "Your ex is nothing, Bethany. A blip on our radar. Seriously, don't stress." He kneels in front of me too and I can't stop myself from reaching out to touch them. Their faces are warm in my palms, their chin scruff scratchy. Both of them close their eyes at my tender touch and my heart feels like it will burst open. I know this isn't love. It can't be. Love takes time and effort. Love takes work. Love doesn't feel as natural as this.

Or maybe it does.

Maybe when you find what you really need in a person and those traits that make you feel validated and safe, then maybe love can swell out of your heart this way. Seconds tick past and I have no idea what to say because my heart is swollen with what feels like love, but torn with the worry about what this relationship will mean.

Then a phone rings and the moment is gone.

Liam pulls his cell from his jeans and answers. "Ryan."

I hear Ryan's voice at the other end but I can't make out the conversation. Callum is watching his brother intently, obviously trying to figure out what's going on too. "Yeah. We'll come right down."

Callum is on his feet in a second and so am I. I don't like the sound of this at all.

"What's going on? What did he say?" I ask resting my hand on Liam's forearm.

"They've got what they need. Now we go and tell Brad to back the fuck off. He's never going to come near you again, do you understand, Bethany. If he does, he's going down for a very long time."

"Please," I say. "I don't want anything to happen to you."

"We're licensed to carry, Bethany. Believe me, it's going to be your ex that gets the shock of his life, not us." Callum smirks and I can see that he's enjoying himself.

There's no sign of concern on either of their faces and I realize that it's just me who's worried.

"Shall I come with you?" I ask.

"Hell no," Liam says. He steps forward to kiss my mouth as though it's perfectly natural, even after all the conversation we've had. Callum does the same, and it does feel natural. It feels like the best thing ever.

"We've gotta go," Liam says. "The twins are waiting, but we'll be back soon. Then we can sort everything out, okay?"

I nod. He makes it sounds so simple and I can see why that is. These men are so capable in their daily lives. They see problems and they solve them, and they don't worry too much about the consequences. I wish I could be more like them.

I follow them to the front door, watching as Callum grabs a big black bag from the table. "Be careful," I tell them as they're leaving and they turn and smile as though they love that I'm fussing over them.

I watch as they walk away and it feels like a part of me is going with them. I know I'm not going to be able to do a thing until they are safely home.

19

CAUGHT BETWEEN FOUR ROCK-HARD PLACES

I get through the next few hours by pure distraction; I use what I find in their cupboards to bake and work on elaborate sugar paste decorations to finish the chocolate cupcakes. When I'm baking I'm usually in a zone but today I can't concentrate. My mind whirs with images of the O'Connell brothers facing Brad. His smarmy smirk and all the bad things his toxic mind could think of to tell the twins. His threats. What he might have already done with the photos.

I know he's a coward - coward of epic proportions - but that only seems to make him more vicious in his vindictiveness and I don't want that turned on my boys.

My boys.

I stop working on the red sugar rose that I'm crafting and take a deep breath. My boys. It feels so right to think of them that way. It feels completely natural to be standing here in their apartment, making them treats and awaiting their return. There's no fear that I'll get hurt. No fear that they'll take hold of my heart and then discard it.

My boys are special. One of a kind. Raised by a beautiful mother who taught them the value of women and the way to handle them with respect and care.

As I think this I feel a wave of peace wash over me. Kerry is right. I need to trust myself and to have confidence that what is in my heart is right and true. I need to let go of the things that don't really matter to me. Mom's opinion. Frank's opinion. The opinion of outsiders who are never going to be important in my life. If Carrie could do it and Katelin too, then why not me?

In my heart I'm as brave as them, I've just had my confidence knocked so much that for a while I forgot who I am, but standing here in this kitchen I feel the realness of me bubbling to the surface. I'm Bethany Blane, the girl who did a bungee jump when she was eighteen-years-old, the girl who ignored her mom and built her dream business, the girl who left a dangerous and controlling man behind because she refused to be miserable anymore.

I'm Bethany Blane who danced on the beach without a care, who swam in the inky black sea at midnight with nothing on.

I'm Bethany Blane and I'm going to be the me that I want to be. The real me.

I rush the rest of the cake decorations and pack everything away leaving four cupcakes on the counter for the men who are out there defending my honor. Then I head to the shower to prepare myself.

Under the water, I feel as though the imposter that Brad shaped me to be is washing away. I use Liam's razor to make myself smooth and after, rub gorgeous-smelling lotion over my whole body. I find my prettiest underwear – a soft pink lace set with panties that tie at the side with ribbon – and put it on. I style my hair and apply natural make-up to pink my cheeks and widen my eyes.

All the time I'm preparing I'm thinking about them coming home. Callum with the dark sparkle in his eyes and his naughty sense of humor. Liam with his light humor and gentleness. Matty with his insight and protectiveness. Ryan with his fierce determination.

Four men who are all so different but feel so right.

Four men who I trust with my life and my heart.

Four men who I'm going to give myself to and damn the consequences.

I slip on a soft-pink silk robe and wait.

When the key sounds in the lock I take one last look in the mirror and stand. Their voices are upbeat. I think it's Callum I hear laughing the loudest. Someone mentions the cakes and then there's a low whistle of appreciation. Mom always said the way to a man's heart was through his stomach. Maybe she was right on that one thing.

I leave Liam's room slowly, head into the open plan area and smile at the sight of four gorgeous men tucking into my cakes. A warmth fills me as I hear one of them moan in delight. It's Ryan who's the first to notice I'm standing there watching. He smiles, scrunching up the cake wrapper.

"Damn, Bethany. You know how to bake," he says. The others turn and I see Liam and Callum notice what I'm wearing. I have no idea what they're thinking. Maybe they're hoping that I'm going to take them to bed and we'll carry on where we left off.

"What happened?" I ask them because I need to know that they're okay and that everything worked out the way they said it would.

"You should have seen his face," Matty laughs. "He shit himself when we turned up on his doorstep."

"He tried to pretend that he wasn't bothered by the fact that we knew all his skeletons but the fucker was sweating," Liam says.

"So what did he say?"

"Not much after we told him that if we find out he's come anywhere near you his life will be over."

"And you think he'll back off."

They all laugh as though the alternative is absolutely ridiculous. "I think his dick climbed up inside his body he was so damn scared," Ryan says.

I shudder at the thought but take great pleasure in adding, "It wouldn't have had far to climb."

They all laugh again. "That's my girl," Callum says and I can feel a blush rising up my cheeks. I look at these men in their snug t-shirts and fitted jeans, bodies, and faces that would make angels fall from heaven just to worship at their feet, and for a moment I don't feel worthy. All my mental and physical preparation hasn't really equipped me for this moment, but at the same time, I know what I want.

They all smile at me as I stand in silence probably looking like a frightened rabbit. I'm angry with myself because that isn't how I want them to see me. I want to be Rio. Fearless and free. I remember the feeling I had when I was spinning in circles on the warm Jamaican sand and it gives me the courage I need. One small step now and I can take what I want.

My hands are shaking as I look down to untie the knot on my robe. The room is suddenly so silent and I imagine four sets of mesmerizing gray eyes fixed on me. I'm wet between my legs and no one has even touched me yet. Just the thought of slipping this robe from my shoulders and standing in front of them in my lingerie is enough to turn me on. I finally get the knot loose and I allow the silky fabric to slide open, parting it with my hands until they can see everything I'm offering up to them.

I look up slowly and the hunger I see on their faces is all I need to give me the confidence to lose the robe completely.

"Bethany," someone says reverently. Who I don't know. Their voices are so similar; low, sexy and masculine.

"Fuck," someone else mutters. This time I'm brave enough to look. Ryan. His gaze is like an inferno; desire's fire licking at my skin. No one moves and I'm left thinking that maybe they need a little something more. I reach to the center clasp of my bra and unhook it.

As it drops to the floor, they all move in unison. One of them is imposing enough. Four is something else. With Liam and Callum, I know the routine. Liam at the front, Callum at the back. With Matty and Ryan now in the picture I have no idea what to expect. They stand around me like four points of a compass. Liam at north, Callum at the south. Ryan to the east and Matty to the west.

"What are you doing, Bethany?" Liam asks. His hand goes to my shoulder and squeezes as though I need reassurance. "You don't have to do this."

"Do what?" I look up and see that his expression looks uncomfortable rather than aroused and for a second I don't get it. Then I realize that he thinks I'm doing this out of gratitude. To repay the debt for them telling Brad to back off. "I know that," I tell him softly. "I want to."

"But you said…" Callum's hands rest on my hips, his whispered words delivered directly into my ear.

"I was scared," I say. "But I'm not anymore."

Ryan's hand goes to my cheek and he turns my head so he can press a kiss on my lips. "I knew you'd come around," he says cockily.

"Oh, you did, did you?" I say. He steps back and tugs his t-shirt over his head with one pull, revealing a chest that would make angels weep.

"I did," he grins. "We're just too much to resist."

Matty chuckles to my left and I turn to him. "Were you so confident too?" I ask, taking his hand and putting it to my breast. His eyes go to where my softness rests against his skin and he groans. "I hoped," he says squeezing gently.

"Looks like your wish came true," I say softly, leaning in to kiss him.

Then I feel hand everywhere. Stroking my curves, gripping and squeezing. Two on my hips, two on my waist. Each breast in the hand of a different brother. Lips on mine; soft and tasting of chocolate cupcake and man. My new favorite flavor. A mouth on my neck, suckling. Lips on my nipple and finally fingers between my legs.

"So wet," Ryan says, and I turn to him, watching as his eyes glaze. His fingers are thick and long, pushing aside my panties, sliding between my labia, spreading me open and pushing inside. I moan as he draws them out slowly, relishing the push and pull, widening my stance so he can get deeper, use more fingers, anything to take me higher.

"My turn," Callum says, and Ryan pulls out. Callum's fingers feel different. Maybe it's the angle because he's penetrating me from behind. Every thrust of his hand brushes something inside me that feels so damn good. Ryan's fingers find my clit and I can barely stand. When Liam latches his mouth to one nipple and Matty to the other I cry out so loudly that I know the neighbors will hear. Fuck. I don't care. It feels too good. Liam gently bites my nipple, sending a current of pleasure between my legs, adding to the sensations his brothers are already building there. Ryan circles my clit slowly, slowly until I'm thrusting against him for more. When Callum puts his hand around my throat and squeezes just a little I come in a rush, sagging against him as wave after wave of violent pleasure washes over me.

"She's perfect," Matty says slowly, licking my nipple gently.

"She is," Liam agrees.

"Whose bedroom?" Ryan asks, obviously eager to get things moving to a whole new level. My pussy clenches at the thought, despite the fact that I just had an orgasm and should be spent.

"Yours," Matty says. "You've got the biggest bed."

Ryan laughs. "Yeah. I was always more confident than you guys."

Liam strokes my face. "He was convinced we'd find someone so we could be together. He was the one that persuaded us to get this place too."

I smile at Ryan. "Looks like you got your wish."

"Not yet I haven't," he says and reaches to pick me up. I squeal as he strides across the room with me in his arm, heading to the door at the far end of the hall. It's open and the room is big. The bed, as promised, is huge. Enough space to sleep us all if we wanted.

"Your palace, Princess," he says, resting me on the comforter. The others come in the room behind him, all starting to shed t-shirts, boots, socks and jeans. I feel like I'm living a dream. I should be so lucky to be with one of these men, let alone all four of them. My mouth is watering at the sight of so much firm chest, perfect muscular thighs, and bulging briefs.

Damn.

I don't realize that I've said that out loud until they all burst out laughing.

"I think she likes us," Matty says, grinning.

"I know she does," Callum says. He's the first to get naked, taking his cock in hand and fisting it until it's rock hard. He drops to his knees in front of me and spreads my legs, reaching to untie the ribbons at the sides of my panties and exposing me to his brothers.

His mouth is on my pussy before I even register his intention, tongue parting my folds and finding my swollen clit with its tip. I lean back, resting on my arms so I can watch what he's doing. I don't get to enjoy the view for long, though. Matty's at my side, stroking my breasts gently, watching as my nipples pucker with excitement. He kisses each one, then my lips too. "I want you so much," he says, licking at the underside of my top lip as his brother laps between my legs. Ryan takes his place on my other side, reaching to hook his hand under my leg so he can spread me open even more.

"I want a taste," Liam says, and Callum moves immediately, letting his twin take his place. I watch as Liam breathes against my pussy, his tongue tracing languid circles around my clit. Oh, it feels so good. Not just the physical contact but also the eyes on me and the intention that is buzzing in the room. Each of these men wants to fuck me and I want them to. So badly.

"I want in first," Ryan says.

"Competitive, much," Callum laughs.

"Listen," Ryan says fiercely. "You've already had the privilege."

"And that gives you dibs?" Matty shakes his head, but he doesn't look angry. There's love in his eyes for his twin and that makes my heart swell too.

"Ryan's always had the least patience," Callum laughs.

"Well, maybe I'll make him wait," I say, raising my eyebrow. Ryan's eyes flash with challenge but he doesn't say a word.

"Matty first," I say, still staring at Ryan. His nostrils flare and I know he's pissed. Riling him up turns me on and I bet if I make him wait he's going to take me extra hard.

Callum tosses Matty a condom and he's sheathed and read within seconds. His cock is long and straight and as thick as his brother. As Liam moves to the side, Matty tells me to shift up the bed. He kneels between my legs and strokes his thumb in my wetness, testing to see if I'm ready. I know I am. When he uses the tip of his cock to probe my labia he can really feel it too. He sinks in deep in one thrust and then holds still. He bends to kiss my lips softly, gently teasing them open and using his tongue to perfection.

Then he moves.

Oh my gosh. Matty does this thing with his hips. There's a twist and grind that feels so damn good I have to close my eyes to drown in the pleasure. Someone takes my right hand and wraps it around a hot and heavy cock. I don't know who it is and I don't care. I love the way it slides in my palm and the feel of the thrusts nudging into the circle of my fists. Matty rises up onto his knees, hooking an arm around my leg and shifting it onto his shoulder. I open my eyes and find Ryan climbing in close, his cock in his hand. I reach out to take hold of it, cupping the rounded head and circling it gently. His eyelids droop and I feel bad that I rejected him before. I want to make him feel good. I want to see him unravel before me just so I can put him back together again.

"I want to suck it," I say to him, my eyes bright with challenge.

He swears under his breath and shifts forward, bringing his dick close to my mouth. I open and he pushes inside gently. God, he feels good. So hot, and salty-sweet against my tongue. I rest my hand on his thigh and I can feel him trembling. Maybe it's the restraint needed to allow me to control the movements. I can guess he must want to thrust so badly, but at this angle, it would be impossible for me to take. Ryan slips his hands into my hair, cupping the back of my neck as he leans over me. Matty speeds his thrusts, his cock swelling impossibly inside me. Hands caress my breasts, pinching gently at the nipples and I groan around Ryan's cock. I feel it swell at the vibrations, and his hips jut forward just a little, hitting the back of my throat. He pulls back then, and I watch as he fists his cock with one hand, fingers seeking out my clit with the other.

"Oh," I moan as the sensations of so many hands and Matty's big cock become too much for me to take.

"Harder," Ryan orders as though he can tell I need more. Matty grips my thighs tight enough to sting and pounds into me. Callum's cock swells in my fist and he tells me if I don't stop he's going to come.

It's the look on his face and the thought of him coming all over me that pushes me over the edge into a flash of orgasm so bright that it's like looking directly at the sun. Ryan slows his finger on my clit to prolong the waves that spread through my body like hot water. I can feel my pulse in my throat and my hands, and then Matty groans as he comes too.

I wish I could see it happen. I wish he'd pulled out and come all over my belly. I wish there was no condom between us and he was filling me up right now. I could put my hands between my legs and feel it leaking out. Matty looks dazed as he grips the base of his cock and pulls out carefully. He leans in to kiss me, nuzzling my cheek and chins with his nose, breathing deeply and making a happy rumble in his throat. "Damn, Bethany," he says and I smile up at him feeling euphoric.

When Matty goes to get cleaned up, Ryan is there to fill his place. "Still want me to go last?" Ryan asks, his voice husky, before he kisses my lips hard. He holds my gaze prisoner, his eyes flashing with challenge. I like this game we're playing. It feels dark and dangerous. A part of me wants him so wound up that he's completely out of control by the time he gets his turn.

I nod and he kisses me again, this time slipping his tongue into my mouth. He kisses like I imagine he'll fuck. Hard, desperate and all-consuming. I slip my hands into his hair, tugging him against me, letting him know how much I want him even though I'm making him wait.

"I think she likes torturing him," Callum says chuckling.

"I think he likes it too," Liam says.

"You gonna get the fuck off our girl so we can make her see stars again?" Callum says.

Ryan rises up on his forearms and scowls. "There's too much fucking talking going on in this bedroom."

"Too much kissing and not enough fucking, you mean." Callum flops onto the bed and sits with his back against the brown padded headboard. He pats his thigh. "You gonna crawl up here, baby girl. I've got something good for you."

I smile as he fists his cock, teasing me with its impressive size. Damn. I'm ready to go again, but who can blame me with four gorgeous men to enjoy. I feel as though I'm finally where I need to be. Surrounded and protected on all sides.

Ryan rolls off me and slaps my thigh.

"Go get him," he says and grins.

I do as Callum suggests and crawl up the bed, taking my place on his lap. He tugs me closer bringing his hands to my face so he can kiss me tenderly. "There she is," he says, tucking my hair behind my ears. "I missed you."

"I missed you too," I tell him. I stroke his shoulder and his chest gently to show him how tenderly I feel about him. Sitting on his lap feels like coming home. I'm so ready that when he raises me up, I slide down on him and it's perfection.

"That's it," he says. "That's where I want to be."

"That looks so good," Liam says and I turn to see the rest of my boys watching me ride Callum.

Liam comes closer until he's kneeling behind me. His hands grip my hips, forcing my thrusts higher and harder. Every impact hits my clit perfectly until I can feel another orgasm rising inside me. "You like fucking my brother?" Liam whispers in my ear. Oh…it sounds so dirty and wrong, but it feels so right.

"Yes," I say.

"And when you're done with him, are you going to fuck me too?" Liam's hands move to squeeze my breasts, pinching the nipples to match the rhythm of my movements.

"Yes," I gasp. "Oh…oh."

Liam slaps my ass and it stings so perfectly. Callum takes hold of my hair in a grip that almost too tight and kisses me like he's a drowning man and I'm his last breath. I feel the same way. Time slips as I'm lost in the motion and moment, eyes closed, body totally given over to pleasure.

"Baby," Callum grunts as he grinds into me hard. "Fucking…fuck."

He seizes, his whole body going tight and I'm right there with him, back arching, mouth in an O shape that reflects my ecstasy. He holds me close for way longer than I'm expecting and to be honest, I'm grateful. Three orgasms and I'm feeling pretty wrung out. My hips are aching and I'm panting like a dog after exercise. After all my gym sessions I should have more stamina than this but I guess it's going to take some time to get used to so much sex in such a compressed period of time. Either that or I'm going to have to schedule them on a rotation of some sort. Not sure how that suggestion would go down.

"You feeling okay, baby?" Liam asks, nuzzling my neck from behind. I nod and Callum releases me from his embrace. I turn and wrap my arms around Liam's neck and he scoops me away from his brother. Liam smells so delicious; cologne and warm skin. A scent that reminds me of vacation and freedom. As he lays me on my back I pull him in close, smoothing my hands over his shoulders and rounded biceps, tugging his hips against mine. "Do you need a break?" he asks, pushing my hair off my sweaty forehead and kissing the tip of my nose. I shake my head because now that he's so close, I want him even closer.

"I'll be gentle," Liam says, nuzzling my neck and stroking my breasts. I glance around and find Ryan sitting the closest. He's holding his cock tightly, his eyes firmly on Liam's hands.

Liam positions himself carefully and begins to push inside slowly. He's so measured and controlled that it doesn't hurt at all. "You're so beautiful," he tells me. "Perfect."

I smile up at him, and he kisses both corners of my happy mouth. His arms go around my back so I'm completely engulfed by his strong form and it feels amazing.

"There he is, Mr. Smooth," Callum says. I can hear the grin in his voice.

"Nothing wrong with a bit of romance," I say, breathlessly. Everything Liam is doing is totally perfect.

"You feel so good," he tells me. "So soft, so warm."

The more he talks, the deeper I fall into this moment. I realize that it's still possible to have moments of intimacy, even when there are others around. It's possible to focus on one person and not at the expense of the others. Liam wants a deeper connection and that's fine with me. More than fine.

His hips grind into mine slowly and firmly, each trust sending pleasure spiking through me. I want to come again. I want him to know how good he's making me feel. I just don't know that I can. Three is a record for me. Anything more would definitely break my brain. The thing is that Liam doesn't seem to be prepared to finish without me. His stamina is admirable. The small of his back is wet with sweat from holding himself back.

"Are you close?" he whispers and I have to shake my head. I used to fake it with Brad all the time but I'm not prepared to do it now. I want the real thing or not at all. I don't want to mislead these men in any way.

"Too much," I say and his mouth quirks.

"Or maybe not quite enough."

I'm about to correct him, reassure him that he's plenty enough for me, then he calls for Ryan and I shut my mouth.

"Get over here," he tells his brother, rolling us onto our sides. I feel the bed depress behind me and Ryan positions himself against my back. A shiver of uncertainty runs through me. What do these brothers have planned for me?

Ryan's hand slides over my breasts, across my belly and hips. Liam moves slowly, hitching my leg up high so he can angle himself right. I feel Ryan's hand move lower and then the press of his cock against my ass. I freeze, waiting to see what he's going to do. I'm not ready for what I think he might be planning. I've never let anyone do that, and Ryan is so big. That would definitely hurt. The rounded end of his cock presses where I was expecting and fearing, and I put my hand on his hip and grip. I think he must sense that I'm scared because he kisses my neck.

"I'm not going to fuck you there," he says. "Well, not tonight. Just let me rub you. It'll feel good."

I'm looking into Liam's eyes and he nods. I imagine what it would be like to experience that and, although I'm fearful, there is a part of me that wants to know what it would be like. I trust them to be gentle, I'm just not ready for it right now.

The brothers fall into a synchronized rhythm of push and withdraw. Liam thrusts deep and grinds against my clit as Ryan rubs at the sensitive ring of muscle that has always been so private for me. It feels better than I could have imagined. After a while I'm rolling my hips, almost urging him to press harder. Liam is swelling and I'm moaning and Ryan is silent and controlled. I'm so close but I just need a little something more. Then Ryan's fingers find my clit and I'm lost. Liam must feel my pussy contracting because he finally lets himself go and rides me through wave after wave of pure bliss. Ryan keeps rubbing and I can't take it…it's too amazing. Too much. Being with these men is blowing my mind, and I still have Ryan left to please.

I make it sound like a chore, but it isn't. It's amazing. Totally amazing to be able to turn and kiss Ryan and make him moan. It's bliss to feel his strong arms come around me, and his teeth nip my neck. It's completely perfect when he flips me over onto my front and spreads my legs wide.

"You wanted to save me until last," he murmurs against my neck. "You got enough energy left to take me?"

I nod, even though I'm feeling a lot like I need to sleep for a month.

He reaches between my legs and touches me gently. I'm feeling sore now but I won't tell him no. He's been patient and now he gets his rewards, and I know I'm going to get mine too.

He cock is resting along the seam of my ass and he shifts until it drops lower to push against my entrance. I'm still so wet from my last orgasm that he slips in the first inch. After that, it's harder, but he's patient. He takes my hair in a rough ponytail and holds it tight, twisting my neck so he can kiss my mouth. It feels so good to be totally at his mercy. It feels even better because I know I'm giving Ryan what he needs.

"Fuck," he murmurs against my lips as he pushes harder and works his way in deeper. His knees nudge my legs open even wider, the weight of his body squashing me into the comforter. I squeeze my eyes shut and moan with every thrust. He's just so big, so heavy, so masculine, that I'm totally overwhelmed. "You love that, don't you, baby?" he pants against my ear, and I nod because I do. So much I want to cry. I feel a hand slip into one of mine, fingers interlacing and holding tight. It happens on the other side too. Ryan lets go of my hair and nuzzles my ear, then kneels up so he can take hold of my hips and pound into me even harder. A hand strokes my hair. Different lips kiss my cheek. Another voice tells me I'm beautiful, perfect, a dream come true.

My heart swells until it feels like it might burst. Knowing they are all there, watching what's happening has me on fire. Remembering how each of them felt inside me while Ryan fucks me is mind blowing. I moan so loudly and it spurs Ryan on.

"That's it, Bethany," he says, giving my ass a slap. Come on my cock." His voice is so gruff by this point and I can't hold it in. I tell him he feels so big, so good, so fucking perfect. I tell them all that I've never experienced anything this amazing before. I tell them that I want them, over and over and over and when I've finished pouring out my soul my body takes over.

"I'm gonna…oh, oh, ohhhh…" I gasp. "I'm coming."

And I do. Oh, I do. Wet as a river, tight as a bow, hot as a raging inferno. I can't seem to catch a breath but I don't care because I know this is it for me. Nothing could ever compare to the way I feel right now, surrounded by the four men who have dropped into my life like a gift and wrapped me up in their embrace.

Ryan isn't far behind me, his cock swelling and pulsing frantically between my legs. I feel his sweat drip onto my back as he leans down to kiss me between my shoulder blades. I turn to kiss him and taste it on his lips. His eyes are half-closed, sex foggy, and sleepy but his smile says it all.

"Fuck me!" he says. "You better be planning on staying, girl, because there isn't a chance in hell that any of us are ever letting you go."

It's been only a few days since I flew to Jamaica to witness my sister take a step into a new life. I wasn't expecting that I'd be doing the same. My heart was bruised and my soul was scarred, but then these men found a way to make me see that I didn't have to feel like that. I could find the way back to myself again. I could be the me I was before Brad crushed my spirit. I could dance on the sand with the wind in my hair and the sound of the ocean crashing in my ears and feel free.

As Callum and Liam, Ryan and Matty help me get comfortable on the bed, drape me with covers and snuggle in around me, I feel like I'm in a dream. Can a person's life drift into snow-globe perfection this way?

Good things like this just don't happen to me, or they didn't until I crossed paths with the O'Connell brothers.

The boys doze and I lie between them, relishing the peace I'm feeling for the first time in my life. They've shown me that my journey can begin again and that they are the perfect travel companions to make my life complete.

I know the road is going to be rocky, but with my twins beside me, I'm certain that everything is going to be fine.

EPILOGUE
4X THE HAPPINESS

3 YEARS LATER

I'm not going to tell you everything has been smooth sailing. Relationships can be challenging when there are only two people involved. Add another three and you have a whole heap of ready conflict just waiting to brew. Especially when four out of the five people are brothers.

Damn.

I never realized brothers could bicker as much as they do.

It's never over anything major, but that doesn't stop it from being really annoying.

Anyway. They more than make up for the sibling stupidity with other benefits! Plenty of other benefits!

After our amazing few days together, Liam and Callum had to head back to Dubai. I cried at the airport and we must have made a very interesting scene. The funny thing was that I didn't even think twice about kissing them both goodbye in public. Any embarrassment or worry about what people would think seemed to have disappeared when I let my own inhibitions go.

They were in Dubai for a whole month and during that time I got to know Matty and Ryan a whole lot better. At first, it felt weird to be with just the two of them, as though I was cheating on Callum and Liam in a way. I know that none of them saw it that way, but I did.

It took a few days for things to feel like they were natural. I got back to business and completed all my orders. Happy customers always make a happy me.

Happy boys too. They love eating all the cake off-cuts and licking out the buttercream bowls. I tease them that they're going to lose their figures, but really there is no danger of that. My boys are gorgeous in every way and only seem to be getting fitter. Maybe it's all the crazy sex that goes on in this place. I swear I've had to take up yoga so I can accommodate all the acrobatics. And my fuffie took a while to get used to so much action.

When Liam and Callum had finally finished sorting out their security contract in Dubai, they came home. And that's when our relationship truly began.

We've had to go through a lot. Mom and Frank returned from Jamaica and the shit really hit the fan. To say there was an angry reaction completely underplays what happened. Amazingly, though, for the first time in my life, I wasn't left alone to defend myself. In fact, I didn't have to say a thing. Matty and Ryan dealt with my mom and their dad. When things escalated to angry phone calls to Dubai, Callum and Liam did the same. Our parents didn't talk to us for over a year. I think it was only the fact that they were getting married that seemed to spur a resolution. By that point, we'd proven our commitment to each other.

Am I glad that we're all now playing semi-happy-families together?

That's debatable.

Having mom in my life in any form is a challenge, but I've tried to be more like Kerry and let things wash over me. I think the fact that both her daughters began to withdraw scared her enough to change some of her ways.

And the fact that there are now five men who have got our backs probably had a lot to do with it too.

There have been interesting reactions from some of our friends.

Disapproval and jealousy from some. We swiftly ignored that.

My friends Carrie and Katelin were very supportive. I guess because they've been through the same situation. Having their backing was vital, and Kerry's too.

Today is a big day.

About a month ago we finally moved from the apartment into a gorgeous house on the outskirts of town. Let's just say it's my dream home. It has enough room that we all have our own space, a gorgeous porch out front, amazing yard and a kitchen big enough to accommodate my baking business. I guess it helps that I have four men bringing home the bacon, and they're pretty damn good at that. It's especially important since we're no longer just a family of five anymore. We have two little additions.

Yes, you guessed it.

Twin boys.

Was there ever any hope that I might have a girl? I think the genetic odds are completely out of my favor.

Caleb and Cole were born last year and they've just found their feet. Now we're all forever chasing them.

Do I have any idea who the daddy is?

Well, the answer to that is yes. When it felt right to be thinking about taking our relationship to the next level, we discussed what that would mean. It didn't matter to me because they would all be my children, and Callum and Liam weren't bothered to know. But Ryan felt strongly that the children we have should know who their daddy is and who their uncles are.

So that's what we did.

Can you guess whose babies Caleb and Cole are?

Callum's. Well, he is the oldest. That seemed the easiest way to decide who'd go first. In a way, I'm glad we did it this way. I got to spend a month making a baby with just him and it felt really special. In some ways, it was weird to have so much intimate alone time but so lovely too.

There is something so totally different about having sex and making love to create a child. A closeness that develops between two people who are forging to build something so amazing together. The others were different around me too. Brotherly almost.

And once we knew I was pregnant, not all of them felt comfortable going back to how we were together. I had to show them that I wasn't breakable and prove that sex isn't bad in pregnancy before they were okay with it. I will confess that after about six months I just didn't feel hugely sexy anymore. Those babies were big and I am not!

We made quite a spectacle in the hospital. The staff just thought that the three big dudes waiting outside were excited uncles. They didn't get the full extent of our connection until all of them burst into the room to congratulate Callum and kiss me. I think the gossip stream was flooded that day!

I know Liam is keen to take his turn. He's been so great with the babies so far. In a way, they are like his own because genetically he and Callum are identical. Caleb and

Cole still get him confused with daddy and I think he secretly likes it.

And I guess this way it means I'm going to be having at least five children…maybe more if the twin thing continues to be so pervasive. Am I finding that prospect a little scary? Hell yeah. Mostly because it's a physical challenge to carry twins. But unlike most women, I have four men on hand to help out, and they really do. The division of labor in this house is amazing. I'm in charge of shopping, laundry, and desserts but pretty much everything else is getting covered by my men.

Diaper changes. Night feeds.

No complaints.

Did I tell you that I think they might be perfect?

Okay, maybe not perfect. Ryan is a covers hog. Matty takes too long in the shower. Callum never turns his clothes the right way before putting them in the laundry basket, and Liam leaves his paperwork all over the place.

But apart from that, I am totally and blissfully happy living with my boys.

So back to today.

We decided that we should hold a housewarming and invite all our friends and family. We have a yard full of hungry people and Matty and Ryan are barbecuing up a storm. Callum's handling drinks and Liam's in full on host-mode. I'm sitting on a blanket with my baby boys, enjoying the sunshine and time with friends.

"So, when are you guys going to start trying for round two?" Katelin asks me. She's bottle-feeding little Isobel and I feel a pang because I know she wanted to breastfeed but can't because of her medical history.

HUGE X4

"Well, Liam said maybe we should start trying in September."

"Ohh…so soon," Carrie exclaims. Her twin girls are currently perched on Ethan and Nathan's shoulders having a water gun fight.

"Yeah. I'm gonna have to fit in two more pregnancies after that so we can't wait too long."

Jenna chuckles. "You're not looking too stressed about that," she says.

"Nah. It's all good." Caleb gets up and toddles off towards Hannah and Dominic. They're his special people. Not godparents because we didn't go that route, but just as good. Dominic hefts him up and throws him in the air. I wince for a second because rough play is still something I struggle with, but Caleb's screaming with laughter.

"So, I've got some news," Jenna says, sounding nervous.

"What?" Carrie is the worst at waiting. She always wants to know everything that's going on in people's lives.

"I'm pregnant," Jenna whispers.

We all lose it. Jenna and Harrison have been trying for years with no success. Something to do with Jenna's ovaries.

"How long?" I say, shuffling over the blanket to hug her.

"Fifteen weeks," she says blushing.

"Oh my goodness." Carrie is hugging Jenna too. "That is just the best news."

"Now I'll have boring baby stories to share with you guys too," Jenna laughs.

"Are you calling us boring?" Katelin says in a mock-angry voice.

Carrie cuts her a glance. "What are you talking about girl? We know we are boring about these kids. Who give a shit about when they've been potty trained or what food they're refusing to eat. I bore myself most of the time."

"True," Katelin says.

"Let's talk about our sexy men," I say.

We all look around to find where they are. Jenna's husband Harrison is talking to Frank, probably about football. It's the universal man-versation.

Carrie's men, Ethan and Nathan, are still getting drenched in the water pistol war.

Katelin's trio, Bryan, Jason, and Austin are serving themselves at the buffet. Katelin laughs. "Look at my three. First at the food. ALWAYS."

"It's cos you keep them so busy," Carrie laughs. "All that sex burns calories."

Katelin gives her a withering look. "These days it's them keeping me busy. I'm so damn tired all the time, but when they start with the moves…well, I find the energy somehow!"

"You're singing my song there, sister," I laugh. "With four of them, even a quickie takes over an hour!"

"Damn," Jenna says. "I mean, I know I lucked out with Harrison but sometimes I look at you girls and wish he had a long lost brother somewhere." She looks over at Harrison and grins. "Don't you dare tell him I said that!"

"He'd probably find it hilarious," Katelin laughs.

"Yeah. Knowing him he'd probably get off on role-playing that out," Carrie says.

Jenna's eyes flash. "Now there's an idea," she says.

Carrie punches Jenna softly on the shoulder. "Damn, that boy's gonna have the time of his life tonight."

"He has the time of his life every night!"

We all sigh because life is good despite all the challenges we've faced. Jenna with her fertility and money worries, Carrie and Katelin with their medical scares, me and the issues with Brad and our parents. We've all come out on the other side, with so much happiness in our lives.

And I guess that in the end it's because we followed our hearts. Not all journeys are easy, but the ones worth traveling are worth the trouble. I scoop up Cole and tell the girls I'll be back in a minute. I head towards Liam who excuses himself from the conversation he's having with my mom to walk with me.

"Thanks for the rescue," he laughs when we're far enough away to be out of earshot.

"No problem," I say. He lifts Cole from my arms and tosses him in the air, making him squeal like his brother. My heart is overflowing with love today. Maybe it's the fact that we're surrounded by our nearest and dearest, or maybe it's just that this life I'm living finally seems to have settled around me enough for me to appreciate it. I'm not sure. But I lean over and kiss Liam tenderly and whisper that I love him.

He obviously senses something because he tugs me against him and kisses my hair. "I love you too, Bethany," he says softly. "So much."

"Shall we try?" I ask him and he knows what I mean right away. His eyes are bright, his mouth quirked into a curious smile.

"Tonight?"

"Yeah."

"You sure you're ready?"

I nod and he beams a full on mega-watt O'Connell smile.

"Babe, I'm gonna make you come so hard tonight," he whispers. "I'm gonna fill you up so many times."

Oh god, the way he talks just hits me straight between the legs. If we weren't entertaining, I'd be dragging his ass upstairs so he can make good on his promise right now.

"You gonna put a baby inside me?" I whisper right into his ear and he shivers.

"Yeah," he says, slipping his hand over my waist to squeeze my ass. "I'm gonna put a baby inside you and I hope it's a girl who looks just like you."

"It'll probably be twin boys," I laugh. "I've already picked out the names."

"Luke and Logan?"

We both chuckle at the tradition that Callum started, using the first letter of his name for his son's names.

"Actually, I was thinking Luke and Lewis."

"Or Laney for a girl."

I smile because it's so damn cute that Liam has already thought about this.

"Laney is perfect," I say and he grins proudly. "Will you look after Cole for a while?" I ask. "I wanna go see Callum."

"Sure," he says. "I'll go change his diaper."

Cole says 'Dada', patting Liam's cheeks and I laugh. "Not Dada," I say. "Lee-Lee."

I turn and make my way to Callum, who is currently mixing up what looks like a mojito.

"Hey," I say, joining him behind the makeshift bar.

"You looking for a cocktail?" he asks, giving me a delicious kiss. He tastes of something sweet.

"You know me. I'm always up for a Long Screw against the wall."

"Well, I can give you one of those later if you like." His smile is dark like licorice.

I wink. "Can you make me one now?"

He laughs. "Sure."

We spend a few minutes joking around while Callum prepares my order. He really is very good at making cocktails. When it's done he pats me on the ass and tells me to go enjoy the party, so I do.

At the grill, Ryan and Matty are looking hot but happy. I swear the whole yard smells good enough to eat.

"You looking for a sausage?" Ryan asks loudly. There are a few sniggers from our friends closest to the barbecue and I snort.

"I think I've had enough sausage to last me a lifetime," I say, putting my hands on my hips. Yet more laughter and grins from my gorgeous men.

"How about some wings, honey?" Matty suggests.

"And ribs," I say. He passes me a plate and I blow them both kisses. It's too hot around the grill to be getting handsy, but I'll make sure I give them plenty of love later.

The party goes on through the afternoon, but the kids get tired early so we're all cleared up by 9 pm. Callum puts the boys to bed and I go up to kiss their sweet cheeks goodnight.

The house is so quiet. Just the murmur of my boys chatting in the den.

I sit at the top of the stairs with my sons sleeping behind me and my men resting in front of me and I know I'm exactly where I'm supposed to be. These boys are my world. The points of my compass. My home and my heart.

After what happened with Brad, I thanked them for rescuing me. None of them agreed that they had. They told me I just needed time and space to see myself and that's what they gave me. Every day I feel another tiny mosaic piece of me fall into place. Now it's not even the pieces that Brad unearthed, but pieces that reflect the new things I'm learning in my life.

I guess the most important realization of all is this: every day that we have time and space to just be ourselves is precious, and finding love that helps on that journey is the ultimate goal of all.

HUGE X4

ABOUT THE AUTHOR

Stephanie Brother writes scintillating stories with bad boys and stepbrothers as their main romantic focus. She's always been curious about complicated relationships, and this is her way of exploring the situations that bring couples together and threaten to keep them apart. As she writes her way to her dream job, Ms. Brother hopes that her readers will enjoy the full emotional and romantic experience as much as she's enjoyed writing them.

Printed in Dunstable, United Kingdom

63835657R00122